{About the Author}

Josephine Bridgers is a graduate of Edgecombe Community College; she has an Associate Degree in Medical Assisting.

The author's passion is writing poems. She has penned several books: Little Mirror, Priscilla's Smile and Child Speak Out! These books highlight the author's growth. Several of the author's poems were featured in The Rocky Mount Evening Telegram.

The author hopes that The Bronze Plantation & Mr. Ed plant a seed and inspire you to educate yourself on the history of this Nation; a Nation that was built on the foundation of free labor. Our heritage is embedded in the soils drenched in blood, sweat, and tears of African American Slaves.

This pain I carry every day
being an African American
in a world that refuses to
Value my worth and accept
The fact that I'm a human
Being Worthy of being free
from oppression

The Bronze Plantation, & Mr. Ed
by Josephine Bridgers

The Bronze Plantation

Captured and sold into slavery

THE BRONZE PLANTATION AND MR. ED

That day was like any normal day for a poor little black girl rich in expectation of a life filled with dreams, so my sister and I took off on our route to my aunt's house, walking, skipping, taking in the scenery, enjoying the cars that passed by and soaking in the breeze. We were little grown-ups only six or seven at the most; we were courageous; because we had at least a two-mile stretch to go. My sister and I giggled, as we chatted about little small things that seemed insignificant but nevertheless pertinent at that time. After walking for a while, it seemed like an eternity, a car full of white kids drove up. Since we hadn't been taught that we need to beware of strangers, we kept on skipping along dismissing their rude comments.

Then one of the older ones, yelled out, niggas do y'all want a ride, this should have rung some type of bell in our heads but we were unfazed by their words, maybe because we had heard this word so many times before especially from our friends and family members. It was like it was the go-to word, Nigga! "Come here Nigga"! You think I'm playing with you niggers. Later on, I would learn that black people used nigga in a different way, it was a slang word and not meant to be derogatory against the African American race. However; white people used this word as a derogatory word that demeans, this young mind couldn't understand.

But getting back to the carload of white youths, my sister and I started walking toward the car, then one of the white teens said; "Get back niggas! We don't ride niggas."

I looked at my sister and she looked at me, what had just happened? Why did they have a mean look on their faces? What did this mean for us? Was this what grown-ups called Hate?

After a few minutes, my mind wondered, thinking about the delicious treats that were at my aunt's house.

Hate, why didn't this five-letter word exist in my mind? After all, I was just a child; I had things to do, like play. All I could think about was fairytales and being a princess. My kingdom was filled with all the beautiful things that a young child only dreamed of. We were almost there, when we noticed the same car of white teens stopping. We slowed down, this time when they asked; "Niggas do y'all want a ride?" We said no and ran like hell.

Whoa! This was a close call, sweat was pouring profusely from our faces.

When my soul cries out, Liberty!
Strength comes to me and restore my
battered body
to a place of solace

{Main Characters in this Book}

{PART ONE}

Massa Pee: The Bronze Plantation Owner, he has three sons: Blue, Larry and Kelly. Blue is the son of a slave; his mother's name is Priscilla. Priscilla was raped by Massa Pee at 13 years old
Massa Pee oldest son Larry, is by his white wife, Grand Lion.
Kelly is the youngest son of all Massa Pee's children by his white wife
Grand Lion is Massa Pee's Wife
The Grand Madame is Calvin and Massa Pee's mother, she was once the head of the clan but she had gotten old
The Grand Madame have three Boys, one son not mention in this book. She has a daughter that she shipped overseas at an early age.
William one of the main characters in this book is a slave; his father's name is Calvin. William is married to Quinita.
White Sapphire is married to Larry, Massa Pee's son
Tom is the white laborer who abused Quinita
Tom the Uncle Tom / the snitch, or was he
Boo Boo: a runaway slave
Kim: the oldest house slave who had a hardened spirit; she had children that were sold off into slavery.

Kelly helped his half-brother Blue escape before the
bounty hunters had a chance to capture him
Millie……………….. The white laborer-midwife for the
white plantation women.
Did Massa Pee have another brother only time will tell.
Josephine is a love interest of Blue
Sapphire (Massa Pee's son Larry's wife)
Second Part of book is about Mr. Ed, a descendant of
William
{PART TWO}
MR. ED…. Patriarch of the family
DELLA……. Matriarch of the family
SEVEN OFFSPRING…….7 girls 4 boy

When life knocks you down,
take the time to exhale
There is so much beauty
Exploding all around us
The beautiful sky, the sun
The rivers, the lakes, the
mountains, the flowers,
the greeneries, the intriguing
people, and most important
of all the generosity of God's
Grace

Harriet Tubman

Best known for being a Conductor of the Underground Railroad

She was an American abolitionist
and political activist.

The Slaves looking submissive
and fearful

{TABLE OF CONTENTS}

Excerpts from Michelle Obama's speech @ the Democratic National Convention

This is the story of this country, the story that has brought me to this stage tonight, the story of generation of people who felt the lash of bondage, the shame of servitude, the sting of segregation, but who kept on striving and hoping and doing what needed to be done. So that today I wake up every morning in a house that was built by slaves and I watch my daughters, two beautiful, intelligent, black young women Playing with their dogs on the White House lawn.

{Frederick Douglass}

"I may be deemed superstitious, and even egotistical, in regarding this event as a special interposition of divine Providence in my favor. But I should be false to the earliest sentiments of my soul, if I suppressed the opinion. I prefer to be true to myself, even at the hazard of incurring the ridicule of others, rather than to be false, and incur my own abhorrence. From my earliest recollection, I date the entertainment of a deep conviction that slavery would not always be able to hold me within its foul embrace; and in the darkest hours of my career in slavery, this living word of faith and spirit of hope departed not from me, but remained like ministering angels to cheer me through the gloom."

{Introduction}

This book is based on the author's feelings, opinions, some truths and her vivid imagination. The author used her imagination to pseudo historical events to bring the readers in that moment. Any resemblance to actual persons, and their location, living or deceased are coincidental, pertaining to The Bronze Plantation and Mr. Ed. However; Mr. Ed portion has some element of truth. The author allowed her readers to visualize the conditions and get a feel of the climate at that time.

Also,this book chroniclize the life of the people living on the Bronze Plantation, the Massa and his slaves. It takes you through the struggles and good times of their individual lives. This book will captivate you; make you interested in the plight and struggles of each individual character. Make sure you introduce yourself to all the characters on the next page of this book. This will help you get to know each person and how they are related to each other.

The second part of this book introduces you to an individual named (Mr. Ed who is a decendant of William a slave). He possess a very high sex drive, a strong personality and lots of charisma; he is a compelling character with charm that inspires devotion in others). It will take you through his married life to Della and the unnessary struggles he placed on his **eleven children.** The last part of the book introduces you to individual stories of the struggles and racism Africian Americans had to endure as they strived to make a life and living for themselves and their families in the United States of America up to this present day.

The author is amazed by the unwavering spirits the slaves demonstrated despite of the inhumane treatment they received. The slaves were unyielding and prepared to stake their claim for freedom at any cost. All they wanted were to live a life from oppression.

The author takes you back to the 1700ths where African Americans didn't have a voice but they never gave up hope. Their spirituality was their comfort and this helped keep them grounded.

The author also thought it was essential to revisit critical events that happened in history that were excluded from the history books purposely to protect the whites people from ever receiving retribution for their hate crimes. The author uses this book as a teaching tool to educate. Let me be clear, all the Massacres cited in this book, happened, but most of these Massacres didn't receive any recognition until later on, when historians and people doing research start demanding the truth. After that extensive research, African Americans found that history had excluded pertinent imformation about black history. Neverthelsess, the author researched to help enlighten herself and her readers about the miscarriage of justice that had occurred and are still occurring to this day. Researchers found disturbing patterns that preceded with every masacre of white mobs killing blacks in 1700ths and 1800ths. The killings were usually incited by white mobs perpetuated by lies to justify killing blameless blacks. This was done because the white folks felt threatened when Blacks became educated and wanted to become entrepreneurs. This incited the whites to come up with a plan, "To Put them in their place."

The majority of the Massacres that occurred mostly always, involved a black man supposely disrespecting or causing harm to a white woman. To add flame to the fire, our history books neglected to mention these events.

After reading this book, the author hopes that the readers will take the time to research some of the events mentioned in this book.

The author paints a clear picture by not leaving anything to chance; she wants the readers to try to visualize some of struggles that the slaves faced. If you think about it, it is mind boggling.

The author researched material that set the tone for the "Story".

This story walks you back into centuries, where black African Americans were bought into slavery and treated as property. It fast-forwards you to the present time where African American are still facing the same old challenges, racist.

Some of the events in the story are difficult to understand. Nevertheless, it was part of the slave's journey.

The author's self-styled is based on imagination along with factual truths.

In reading this book, the author hopes that you leave away with, compassion and become appreciative of all human life. The roles of the slaves helped shaped the path allowing us to demand changes in a broken system. It is the author's hope that this will inspire you to demand only the best and not be passive when it comes to things that affect your well-being. Maybe, it will ignite "a sparkle" causing a flame that will propel you to get off your behinds and take action.

After the author witnessed on television, the insurrection that occurred, January 6, 2021, her conscience overwhelmed her to take actions by using her writing as a platform to educate. And if we are not careful, democracy will slip away and we will be back to *square one.* " Watching the 2021 insurrection the author decided to complete her book. She cuddled her thoughts for years before she was called to action. Then she was compelled by her conscience to take action. She realized that progress skates on a thin ice. The nation saw the President of the United States, number 45, incited a riot. Then waited in the White House, the people's house, when the insurrection occurred. He gloated about what was happening to our capitol. It was reported that he was elated.

Never in history had there been a blatant disregard for democracy from a President who was voted out of office by the people. That's why it is so critical that we don't become complacent because democracy isn't guaranteed to us.

Your contribution costs nothing only your energetic voice is needed to spear head future growth. Dig deep inside the hollow core of your heart to find, the power you need. A leader's goals are dictated by their actions and their mere existence makes them willing to fight. It is an unexplainable desire that propel them to a higher standard to do something. It's a desire and a willingness to attain and demand changes because few people are cut with the thread that interlace together to demand changes.

Another example of a hero is, the ability to fight when the path is blocked with distracting obstacles but they are willing to see beyond the depth of pain and they show a willingness to fight for causes regardless of the outcome. This requires months or even years of strategizing, while facing challenging tasks.

This book walks you back in time where freedom was bought and paid for by the innocent blood of blacks. They were willing to fight for that sporadic glimpse of freedom by plummeting head first while hoping to settle on their feet. These people were willing to die, in the hope that one day their scarred body would heal its wounds after crossing the freedom line. Where the big, little and weighed down would be able to stare up   in the sky and say "I sir free man! I sir free woman!"

Some of the characters in this book are fictional but nevertheless, the author tried to depict what the key players went through during slavery.

THE BRONZE PLANTATION AND MR. ED

The author tried to include important details relating to what transpired by researching material and making sure she included pertinent points. Even though this story is an imaginary depiction of what happened, some of the events are factual. The slaves endured cruelty for no other reasons other than to build wealth for white people, and to build up this country so that white people would be the only race of people to gain wealth which would be passed down from generation to generation. The white race enjoyed and benefited from black labor for centuries. They used our skin color as a stigma for this purpose. Also, this story paints a picture of how the Massa dictated his authority.

When the slaves arrived in America, they had no rights, their rights had been stripped from them. They were subjected to inhumane treatment and the journey they faced had just begun. As a race they may've been destined to be destroyed, but faith kept them afloat. Kidnapped from their native land, they were brought to America shackled like animals awaiting to be slaughtered, and then they were sold into slavery by the highest bidder. Family was torn apart.

Some of the inhumane treatments included: being shackled, lynched, mutilated, amputated, or castrated, sexually assaulted, mocked, tortured with instrument fitted on head, rubbing pepper, salt or other hardened substance on their wounds, brutal whippings, and branding with the branding iron. This inhumane treatment aided as a reminder of the price these brave slaves had to pay in order for them to reclaim their dignity propelling them to fight for freedom at any cost. Whether it meant dying, being wounded, beating or amputation, they were willing to fight for it, despite of what they told; they knew it was their God given pride to live as a free soul. Can you even imagine, kidnapped and brought to another country to serve the white man? Chained like animals, the Africans were stripped of their dignity. Family was separated; they had to work and received no pay.

The main purpose for slaves being kidnapped and brought to this country was **free labor**. Things we take for granted like going places, we want to go, eating what we want to eat and being able to basically do what we want to do. Slaves were denied these basic rights.

When the opportunity came for them to seek freedom, they ran and didn't look back. Terminology used, for these slaves' seeking freedom, "freedom seeker." Slaves had people helping them on their journey. They were called conductors; they helped the slaves on their path to freedom. Most of the conductors provided safe houses where the slaves could hide until a clear path was provided. Another term is critical, "maroon", these were the runaway slaves who had escaped. We must salute the slaves' efforts on their journey. And never forget where we came from by reminding ourselves that oppression and the rugged road to redemption is still a ladder, we must closely climb every day. Because we don't want to go back to a time and place where freedom rang but oppression tripped us down.

Some of the characters portrayed in the story and Mr. Ed may intrigue you because of their similarities to the threats we are facing today. That's why we must keep the torch lit and not get so complacent with our lives.

If we slip for one second, there will be more troubling events, like what happened on January 6, 2021. This riot (insurrection} had been boiling over for years and it finally came to a head. It showed us what racist people will do to stay in power. This tragic event was dumped on our laps for us to analyze and wonder who and why. The insurrection questioned our moral duty and planted a seed of doubt, letting us now know, we have not overcome. The fight is not over.

We witnessed a disgraced President, incite his followers to go and steal democracy before our eyes. This caused a domino effect resulting in lives lost and some injured because number 45, refused to accept defeat. He wanted to hold on to power, regardless of the damage it was doing to our democracy only for his personal gain.

We aren't shacked like the slaves but rest assured we are still oppressed. Today, *we are still sick and tired of being sick and tired.* We continue to face disparities in the courts, jobs, housing, banking and the list goes on. The author tailored the story to give insight to some of the problems the slaves faced which is paralleled to what we in the twenty first century are facing today.

This book hopefully will help its readers become more educated and make a change in their life by becoming more active instead of being submissive to causes that have a huge impact on their lives.

Sometimes we need to address a problem before it has a chance to take up root. The author followed the story and let it simmer for years before heating it up and planting it in her thoughts. Then she waited for it to explode like chocolate pudding, bursting through barriers leaving a flavor not impeding our thirst.

In writing the story, the author used her imagination to bring to light, what life was like being oppressed, belittled and dehumanized to the point of shame while silenced from speaking the ill fate that was occurring from the oppressors.

{Acknowledgement}

Thanks to the creator God because everything originated with him. I would like to give thanks to having such loving parents, Eddie and Odell Jenkins who are now deceased; they helped me appreciated life by showing me the tangible gift of love. My mother had a thirst for kindness and didn't ask anything in return. She looked forward to God's Kingdom one day, where God's mercy will rain and there will be no pain. My father was a jokester; he used to tell stories and all of the children gathered around listening intensely. That's where I developed my passion for story-telling. I was amazed at the level of knowledge my father had. My parents' love was entrenched in me and they both had great work ethics. They instilled this in me. Also, I would like to acknowledge my husband, Calvin Bridge and my children; Larry Hill, Michael Hill and Kimberly Hill. These four people are the love of my life. My siblings: Gidget Seaborne, Diane Whitaker, Earnest Jenkins, Geraldine Jenkins, Maggie Jenkins and Lillian Jenkins, best siblings! We have had our differences like siblings, nevertheless, we love each other. My aunt and uncle, they are both deceased now, Carrie and Jack Harrison. They were both beautiful souls that provided me shelter when I went to stay with them and they asked nothing in return. They treated me like one of their children. I will never forget their outpouring of genuine love. A special cousin, Bettie

Harrison, she pushed me with my writing. Telling me, "You don't have to rush, 'take your time with your craft."
Special thanks to: Gloria McKenny, who worked as an educator for over thirty years in Baltimore Maryland, she helped with the editing of The Bronze Plantation and Mr. Ed along with my daughter, Kimberly Hill.
A niece that passed before the completion of this book, Carolyn Johnson Fields. She was a loving soul and will be missed. Also, special thanks to Jaimi Boston for formatting.

{Synopsis}

The author gives you a sneak preview of what it was like to be a slave in the 1700s & 1800s
Slavery in the United States was the legal institution of human **chattel slavery, comprising the enslavement primarily of Africans and African Americans, that existed in the United States of America from its founding in 1776 until the passage of the Thirteenth Amendment in 1865.**

Since historians excluded some key events, and neglected a lot of black contributions, the author was compelled to research about her history and report her findings within this piece of literature. Even though some of the events in this book is fictional, the author set a tone for what it was like being a slave.

The author highlighted some of the massacres because she felt historians had excluded them purposely. Some of the slaves struggles, sadly, we are plagued with today. But under a different scenario white people using their power to hold on to a shrinking power, we saw that blatantly on January 6, 2021 with the insurrection. Trump incited a mob and tried to overturn the will of the people to stay in power. Racism just didn't start with Trump but he used his clout to stir up a fragile system that was already embedded in racism. White Supremacy has always had its roots in our government. The author stressed the importance of researching history so we will not become complacent to avoid a repeat of the tragic event that has plagued American and denied Blacks the rights that whites are readily afforded.

To live free from oppression is still not a luxury afforded to African Americans even today.

{Chapter One}

Massa Pee's Plantation and his Slaves

The Bronze's story is an informative story that was passed down to the Williams's family for centuries or more. In a time when the slave women were supposed to be compliant to their mates, they showed the utmost respect. It was usually the woman that kept the family going. The story is about the struggles and the pain the slaves faced on their journey to see over yonder; where black and brown men and women would one day be able to gaze up at the sky and say, "I sir am free!"

The story introduces you to some main characters with their unique personalities, nevertheless, they all played a role in helping to overcome obstacles, while animals were treated better than the slaves.

Little William had found favor in Massa Pee by becoming one of the strongest youths and he was the spitting image of Massa Pee's brother, Calvin, but he was jet black. When Little William smiled, he displayed his beautiful pearly whites; they sparkled like diamonds. Little William had a best friend named, Blue; they both were inseparable, after all, they were kin, produced by two highly respected plantation owners. Being pale skinned, Blue enjoyed more benefits than William. Blue was built just like Little William, huge with a sculptural body that took years for even a full-grown slave to acquire.

William and Blue grew up on the Bronze's Plantation, one of the biggest Plantation in the South at that time. The Bronze's Plantation was bronze because Massa Pee enlisted foreigners to design the plantation like no other, with every effort placed on carving fixtures out of bronze and all the furnishings in the planation were made out of marbles. Massa Pee also used gold to highlight the centerpieces with extravagant touches. It was the most spectacular planation in the entire region.

Little William and Blue grew to become the sturdiest men, with bodies sculptured to perfection. There were no other slaves anywhere built like these two. Both of these young slaves could do the work of ten or more slaves; they worked effortless while other slaves had to struggle. Williams's muscles bulged out under his garment because it seemed none of his garment fixed him, if he was living in today's society, his pants would be called high waters.

Blue's eyes were bright as the starry sky, they had a calming effect on the young slave girls, just like the clouds in the sky. William was mixed blooded also, but his skin color led people to believe he was only from slave descendants.

Massa Pee was Blue's father and this saved Blue on several occasions after missing the deadline, proclaiming that all slaves had to be in before the sunset.

On one occasion, he was in the woods doing what he did best, knife throwing. And he was good at it, so good that he could hit something right in the bull's eye. Massa Pee talked to Blue the first time he was caught, but the next couple of times, Blue felt the rage of his father after getting a good old fashioned tail whipping. But this didn't stop Blue, he got caught again.

Another occasion, Massa Pee saved Blue, it just so happened that Massa Pee was just around the corner when he came riding by on his favorite horse Midnight when he saw the noose around Blue's neck. He pulled out his rifle and shot the horse dead, leaving Blue dangling in the air before Massa Pee ordered a bounty hunter to cut him down. Blue fell on the ground gasping for air. Time after time, Blue was saved after the bounty hunters recognized that he was Massa Pee's slave.

Then, there was one time a new bounty hunter was in the region, the dogs sniffed Blue up a tree; Blue's mouth was filled with berries when he heard dogs and bounty hunters surrounding him, Blue had almost got himself lynched again.

The bounty hunters were very disappointed that Blue had been saved. Because one of them was itching to hang another black slave, this he did as a sport. Blue and his friend William grew into handsome young slaves. They had their pick of the young slave girls.

Even the white madams began to notice Blue and William. There was one woman in particular, Sapphire, she was Blue's half-brother Larry's wife. Sapphire used every opportunity to get next to Blue. She would summon him to her quarters when her husband went on his trip. Blue would bring her wood for her fireplace and she would watch from the balcony while he cut the logs. Then, she would slowly watch him bring the logs inside the quarters, lusting with every breath. And when he entered the room, she unrobed, exposing her naked body, letting her blanket fall to the floor. Blue told William about Sapphire, and William told him, "Blue, "don't do it." 'Because once you take a bite of the fruit, there is no turning back." They laughed.

Massa Pee made William the overseer of the entire planation, his role on the plantation was more important than Blue. But Blue never mind, William knew so much, it was like he was born to **lead.** Sapphire's eyes were hazed, and she had long blonde hair that hung down her back almost reaching her rear end. She was one of the most attractive white women that Blue had ever laid his eyes on. Blue was used to sweaty field slaves with wooly hair when he had his sexual encounters with them. These encounters usually happened in the middle of the night; he had the most satisfying encounters with one black beautiful young slave girl. Blue was starving for the desire of the flesh, in the raging heat, he gave another workout, but this was great, while his flesh drenched with sweat, afterward he told the young slave girl, it was a pleasure to have her for that night. In contrast, Sapphire was white as snow. She was exquisite, she looked the part of royalty. Blue had never seen a white woman that beautiful in his entire young life.

The next woman that had a chance against her was his best friend, William's lady, Quinita. Quinita was the opposite of Sapphire; her skin was black as night but every feature on her face was positioned to perfection. Her eyes sparkled like the stars in the heavens. And her shape, well, it had poor William fighting almost every day because all the other slaves were fighting for her affection. The white women tormented Quinita; they were jealous of her majestic beauty. There was a slight difference though,

Sapphire was a white woman with everything. She had money; lots of money and she had the luxury of living a life of privilege because she lived on Massa Pee's plantation where she was surrounded by servants. They bathed her white skin, showering her with perfumes of all scents, and cooked whatever she wanted. She didn't have to lift her hand for anything. Sapphire's perfumed body smelled like a rose garden surrounded by the aroma of lilies. Was Blue the only slave looking at Sapphire, heck no! She was known for selecting the best slaves for her appetite, then moving on but she liked Blue more.

Blue was hooked on Sapphire and he begin to plot every wakening hour to be with her; meanwhile, his friend William plotted to escape. Kim rushed to help Quinita.
Massa Pee's son had a fetish for young slave girls.

Before they reached puberty, Massa Pee's son, Larry indulged his cravings forcing his manhood on the young slave girls until blood was shed. He had to taste their virginity. Most of the slaves hid their children's age from him to avoid finding their child drenching in blood almost dead from his violent attack. But he didn't want anyone to look at his wife Sapphire, if anyone did, he shot them dead. He was a bad, bad man!

Getting back to Blue, no one could work the field, gather corn, and turn up the crops better than Blue. But Blue had seen this white green-eyed lady naked and he had to taste the fruit, even if it meant getting bitten by the snake or the lynch rope. Sapphire had captivated him. But was it worth dying for? He didn't know. Then a question is posed, was Blue willing to give up his life as a secret runner? Time will tell. How long would he be able to hide this forbidden love from the other slave' women who had fought *tooth and nail for his attention*. While he slipped in the heat of the night with Lady Sapphire. There was something about Sapphire that intrigued him more and more. Poor Blue, he ignored his grandmother pleas to stop before the master gets hold of this and hang him. He tried to stop, but Sapphire had a hold on him and he couldn't shake it loose even if it meant death.

Meanwhile, he had to convince his grandmother he had no interest in Sapphire but he knew his grandmother had a sense he was lying. He secretly plotted more encounters because the white flesh against his only intrigued him more. Now they called for him," Come, Come"! He surrendered his powers and now he was powerless to stop his due reckoning.

William had his own problems; he was dealing with his quest for freedom after witnessing one of his master laborers, raping his prize possession, his dear Quinita. William was chopping firewood with his right hand when he heard loud noises, he realized it was Quinita. She was crying out. Oh, there had been other victims that William was too ashamed to admit. Nevertheless, he witnessed more while only a child, he watched in horror, while witnessing his sister Isabela being raped by his playmate Massa Pee friend's child, James. William was frozen, he was afraid to help. But this time, it hit his heart string and pulled all the delicacies leaving them exposed to all who observed this brutal attack. Powerless, William ran and ran until his bruised feet reached the lake as he stumped to wash away the shame, while the blood fell profusely from his legs. When he stopped, his shirtless skin was covered with pine cones, leaves and insects bites. Why couldn't he stop them? Was there any mercy for his woman, who he had abandoned and left to fend for herself? Was this the duty of a coward who had lost his manhood years ago?

Nevertheless, he screamed and shouted before God, this is my destiny, I am a Man, God give me strength to just walk tall and reclaim my manhood.

Quinita continued to cry out asking for help while the other women walked away, they screamed, but provided no help. Quinita lifted her eyes up toward the sky, and prayed. She knew they all had been victims of this brutality in one form or another. She had heard the screams and now it was her turn to fight the blue-eyed demon called the white man.

Kim the oldest slave on the plantation comforted Quinita

Kim the oldest and the most rebellious woman on the plantation hurried to aid Quinita. Never mind that she might get killed, this reckoning was not hers to claim. She couldn't stand to see her fellow slave go through this alone, oh, hell no! What if she got lynched? No chains or whips would stop her from rendering aid to her fellow slave, oh no, it did not bother her no way no how. She had been beaten until her body fell to the ground and she kissed the dirt and spit it out but Kim refused to cry out in pain or wet her lips in shame. James was about to strike her but Massa Pee's son motioned, "She is my best cook and housemaid. Don't touch her"! Kelly yelled. He had just ridden up and he knew Kim would die rather than submit to being beaten by whips and chains. Massa Larry knew this, but he didn't care. When Massa Pee left, he told the white laborers, "Don't Touch Her, if anyone touches Kim, I will shoot them on the spot". Kim raised her eyes and sang her favorite song; God, please lift me up and let me fly.''

She gathered Quinita in her loving arms and carried her to her quarters and nursed Quinita's bruised body. She washed Quinita's clothes and placed medicine on the whips. She comforted the young woman by singing a song of praise to the one who gave her the courage to walk away instead of being killed like so many others. William was so distraught, he fell down on one knee, he prayed for strength because how can you not be broken despite what the Massa thought, he knew he was a man. As the rage came out, He yelled and screamed.

Now was the time to reclaim his purpose. He would devote his life protecting Quinita.

With no shoes to soften the feel of the rocks or whiskey to numb the pain that wedged deep into his heart, he yelled out in agony as he held his bleeding heart. He was ready to strike anyone, beat someone with his bare hands until they bled. Until then, he mourned for hours before he collapsed on the ground. There he sucked on the dirt, like a newborn calf, he hungered for his sweet Quinita.

The Massa's friend had laughed and mocked poor Quinita while she glanced at William in complete desperation. She realized he was helpless but an angel came and gathered her clothing. Even though she was beaten down she refused to be broken, she refused to give them the satisfaction of knowing they had wounded her. She smiled a halfhearted smile while holding on to Kim as they walked away with pride and grace. The two hugged each other while they sang and asked God to give them renewed strength.

Quinita was taught by her parents that even if someone beat and bruise your flesh, they *can't touch your soul.* Her mom said, "This separates you from all the other creatures on this earth, the soul of a human can't be bought, because it was paid for in blood."

Quinita knew in her heart she was a person of value and nothing that they could do to her that would make her devalue her self-worth. Then it seemed like a light glowed around her in the dark as dust flew in the laborer's eyes from the wind, the dust seemed to come out of nowhere. The slave owners' eyes were covered with sand while they fought each other in blind desperation. The white laborers started throwing up, it was just so weird. The laborers were too drunk to realize they were hurting each other. Was it something different? These slaves had never witnessed this before in there many years of being a slave on Massa Pee's plantation.

These white men were acting like fools. Was the white man's God finally looking down and finally saying, enough is enough?

Quinita walked up to the man that had raped her with a smile and tuned out the most spiritual song. "God if this is my journey, my life is your temple. Looking confused, he murmured something stupid and walked back to the plantation. Oh, she knew what he had did, but she wasn't afraid

After all, slaves were property so that meant the white man could do whatever he wanted.

William was mixed blood, even though he was darker than most mixed blood slaves. It wasn't any denying he was Calvin's son, he looked just like him down to the mole on his upper lip.

William began to weep, not for Quinita, but for himself. A coward that was not able to comfort this brave woman who had a heart spirited with the strength of lion. Quinita had the soul of an angelic warrior.

Her skin was like being in a bed of roses. William didn't talk to Quinita about what had happened, all his energy was centered around escaping Massa's Pee's planation. After years of William being submissive to a man that had spurred out broken promises, telling William

every year, if he worked hard, he would free him and his wife. But William had to be careful, usually after a rape that occurred often, the black slaves were observed more because the white owners and overseers deemed them a threat. So, the mean overseer who raped Quinita watched William because he saw the hate in William's eyes. The mean old overseer knew he had to watch that boy.

Meanwhile, William had started planning his escape and he had spoken to the old slaves and had gathered all their wisdom and he condensed it for safe keeping. Quinita wasn't broken; she stood beside her husband and was proud because what those animals did to her, in her heart, she knew one day that the Lord would make them pay. But not before she grinded up something for that nasty **sicko**'s meal.

The master had sold one of her sons and now he was giving her daughter the eye. Quinita's daughter was only twelve years old. Plus, Quinita had heard from the housemaids that the next holiday Massa Pee would be selling twenty more slaves.

William continued to teach his boys how to survive the rocky terrain and Quinita prepared the girls for the demanding travel. Quinita made giant sized dolls for the bed in case the overseer came to check on the slaves at night. She had instructed her friend of what to do, the overseer was infatuated with Quinita's friend. He came almost every night and got her out of the bed with her mate, just to have his way with her. This became a ritual; the poor slave didn't have any choice in the matter, so when Quinita told the young slave woman what she wanted, the brave girl jumped in line. That night, when William and his family was leaving Massa Pee's plantation, it was her job to get the dirty old overseer out of the way. She was to come out that night and get him to go in the woods with her, this task was easy. Then she waited to get a signal like usual, it was in the form of bird calling that was the signal she could return to her little shack. Williams's boys had developed into strong young men and it was almost time for the White Ball; the long wait was almost over for their planned escape.

Now that William's eyes had opened, he was bout to do whatever it took to stake his claim at becoming a free man. Freedom! Freedom where a man could claim that right. What constitutes a man, why am I treated less than what I am? I am a Man! Not a Boy. He screamed loud! What Constitutes Being a Man! I would have rather died in my mother's belly, than to be bursting with defeat, I couldn't help the woman whom I love. I' sir screamed, and screamed but no one heard me, how long, how long, my Lord? The smell of slavery pollutes my mind dousing my heart with ignominy (shame)

Raping and torturing innocent beings for sport entertainment, only debase God's name. I gotta go, I gotta go, if I don't, they will break me and I will never be able to claim my prize, Freedom. Where is the victory my Lord? Is it tucked away in the Massa's shed?

People beaten, shamed and killed; this heavy price tag for freedom isn't theirs to own or claim! But whether I succeed or not, it is my fate to pave the way for the next warrior waiting to be born. I'm troubled! I scratch my body until it bleeds trying to remove the stench of the foul odor from the air, coming from the cowards who had tortured my sweet Quinita. Silence calls my name from the grave. Only cowards, not men, enslave and promote this type of violence. My soul cries out, Freedom! Freedom! Why do they want to take what is not owed to them? My soul aches for some sort of vengeance. I welcomed it, but it mocks me, enticing me like a harlot, Come, come then disappear. Now I have a new set of eyes, this new revelation of freedom, I now embrace; it echoes deep into my guts bleeding for vengeance. Saying it's time y son, raise your voice and take your claim! Now that your senses have been awakened, you can demand with your voice some changes. They only let you see into the depth of their souls to satisfy their depraved appetites because what's born from the fruits of Love can't be contained in a cage

Boo Boo was another slave that tried to warn William, but he wouldn't listen

William regretted doing everything the master asked, did he have a choice?

After years of obeying the Massa's demands, it was time for William to reconsider what his position was, being that he was an overseer of all the slaves on Massa's plantation. What would be his next move? With his heart shattered, what would he do next to reclaim his dignity as a man and as a companion to Quinita? He heard the call from the wilderness to wake up his sleeping conscience and now *an eye for an eye was about to occur*. It was time for William to pave the path to freedom and time for a new blood line to take the helmet and fight the fight on his new found awakening. He was about to become a freedom fighter. It was on that hot humid day; another freedom fighter was born. Bathed in the innocent blood of Quinita, after witnessing her being raped, his blood boiled for retribution. He gritted his teeth as he watched the spectators as they fought each other while they satisfied their urges. Now someone had to pay; so, he kicked and kicked the big tree, he kicked until his feet bled, he kicked and kicked until all his power and all his strength forced the big tree to fall backward, bloody from his blood, the hurt had finally dissolved. He was free. William didn't know his father as a man because he was never around, he was always overseas.

After weeks, then months, William never forgot the onlookers of white bearded men mocking Quinita. While they abused her and taunted him to intercede in the hope to tie another slave to a tree for sport games, he didn't submit to the pressure. The white laborers hung slaves up and tortured them every fourth Sunday for sport games

These owners knew Massa Pee was gone and this was their opportunity to touch something that Massa Pee didn't have the heart to do. They knew this was the perfect time to act now before the return of Massa Pee.

Boo Boo started running after talking to William, stupid fool, William thought the Massa loved him, he was only another Uncle Tom

Getting back to the overseers, they knew they had to come up with a lie and they were ready to fill Massa Pee's head with all sorts of lies bout what happened, after all, who was Massa Pee gonna believe, a slave or white men? William became a harden soul; he strategized every move he made from that point on, he revisited his thoughts when he was approached by a runaway slave, who asked him for help. William laughed at Boo Boo, saying "we have it good here, 'the Massa treat us fine." Poor runaway slave, Boo Boo, he just shook the dirt of his trousers and took off running, ain't no need to waste any talk on a fool. Gotta go before Massa Pee found out. William watched as Boo Boo fled for his life, he felt sorry for Boo Boo. He didn't understand why he wanted to leave Massa Pee's Plantation. They ate well, sure they worked hard, but isn't that what slaves supposed to do, what was Boo Boo's problem? Later on, William heard that Massa Pee had sold two of Boo Boo's children. This made Boo Boo mad, he was so mad, he beat up another slave for asking what's wrong. Boo Boo never got mad about anything. I guess when it came down to your folks, the anger comes out. Boo, Boo ran off that night with his whole family escaping to the Underground Railroad. Oh boy, now William understood, he would never be considered a man

in the eyes of the white man. After that day, Boo Boo's son got sold to the highest bidder, he was very infuriated. Who would be next?
His daughter could be next, so he started preparing for the big escape. He had put aside additional clothes for the journey and told some kin he was leaving. Boo Boo who was once lively now he was quiet, he only talked to his mate. Massa Pee didn't mind what went on, just as long as he put in good work. Boo Boo's son was sold off at the ripe age of thirteen. This was Boo Boo's pride and joy. This hurt him down to his bones. It prompted him to seek refuge to protect his family. Boo had another child sold off when the child was a baby. He used to be just like William. He believed everything that the master told him about freeing him and his family.

The master told him that for years. "Boo Boo, if you work hard, I will give you your paper at the end of the year." And every year he waited and waited, but Massa Pee never gave him free papers for him and his family, "I'm a man" Boo Boo said one day and I refuse to be kept like an animal any longer. He had to run and provide a safe place for his family. His eyes had been opened, he was willing to put in the work and freedom was his goal. But before Boo Boo left, he was bout to touch Massa Pee's prize possession, his horse, Midnight. Boo Boo had to inflict pain somewhere, sadly it had to be that way. His family was devastated when they learned the master was planning on selling his youngest son. What could he do? He was Massa Pee's property. His wife cried and cried. He was powerless. The slave trade didn't care if a family was being torn apart. Months after the master was celebrating his big sale, Boo Boo and his entire family was slipping away with the few possessions on their quest for freedom. Boo Boo gave Massa Pee's horse Midnight a dose of critters poison, but he didn't stay to watch the horse demise. Boo Boo's family huddled together and said a prayer before they left. They thanked God for their health and his mercy. They sang their favorite song, **Swing Low Sweet Chariot.** Despite their burdens, they believed God was gonna walk them through the rain. Boo Boo and his family fled from Massa Pee's plantation that night. They did this for their son who had been sold and because they wanted to remain a family. Boo Boo traveled along the river banks looking up in the sky, he followed the stars on his way to a safe house. A place he could rest and build up his strength on his quest for freedom.

The path to freedom wasn't gonna be easy, but he had to try. His family's survival depended on him. Nothing was gonna stop him because he was willing to move every stone to protect what was his. The night was gonna be long, they didn't get no sleep because they had to move fast before Massa Pee woke up. Boo Boo knew Massa Pee was gonna come for him with everything he had. Before he left, he traveled back and forth, planting his clothes in different locations to fool the dogs and divert the scent. Then Boo Boo used the river route because the dogs couldn't pick up their scents once they were in the water. Boo Boo was so fast that he was able to reach a safe house the next morning before the master ate his morning meal.

<u>May God, Grant You Peace</u>! Was the signal for the person on the other end to let Boo Boo and his family in the dimly lit building? Now Boo Boo was on his journey, a path to freedom. He was bout to come in contact with freedom fighters, slave owners, freed slaves and lawyers. Every one of these people led him a little closer to the Underground Railroad.

Blue's mother Priscilla dies at thirty-eight.

After Boo Boo tried to get William to help him but William refused. He knew that it was a matter of time before William felt the fire from the master dark side. He didn't have the time to school William on the next chapter, so he ran. How foolish was he to think William would help him? He ran because he knew his life depended on it. Boo Boo had seen Massa's snitch, watching, pretending to shine some of the Massa's shoes. The Uncle Tom name was Tom; Tom told the Massa everything. Sadly, he didn't care if he was selling out his own kind; that's why his wife ran off with another slave ten years earlier. She got tired of Tom kissing the Massa's behind but was Tom a snitch? On the outside, it seemed so, but Tom had a secret. Tom masqueraded as an Uncle Tom to fool Massa Pee, sure there were some causalities that Tom had to snitch on to appease Masa Pee so he could trust him, and Tom did this with regret. Unbeknownst to the other slaves, Tom was one of the main conductors of the Underground Railroad. He had learned all the safe routes from someone you would never expect, Calvin, Massa Pee's own brother. Calvin had moved to England because he had developed a distaste for the Slave

Trade, he tried his best to hide it and when it became too much after witnessing so many brutal beatings, he was done; he just left without telling anyone but his mother.

While in England, he hooked up with some key players that were part of the Underground Railroad. He used his money to help slaves find safe houses. And when it came down to his son William making a move to escape, he came back personally, and made sure the other conductors knew that this slave called William needed to be protected at all cost.

Massa Pee never found out about his brother's role in the Underground Railroad. Calvin knew his brother would do everything in his power to save the Slave Trade and protect what was his.

Tom knew that William was Massa Pee's nephew. That didn't make a difference. William's blood had slave in it, and he knew that no matter what, William was just a slave in Massa Pee's eyes. Tom was a hard-working slave, even though he was well into years it was getting harder for him to determine who would live and who would die. It was necessary to protect the Underground Railroad, so Tom acted his part as a snitch and lived his life in secrecy. As he got older, it became harder to choose who was deserving and who would break if given the chance. This weighed heavy on his mind. That is why he wore this band of shame not because he wanted to. It was because he felt it was his duty to give the young ones that hope that one day, they would be free! No more good slaves, only a man. Tom walked slowly over to Boo Boo's tiny shack, it was quiet, but before he could open the door, he was met by a fist. Before he knew what happened, Boo Boo was throwing blow after blow knocking Tom on the ground here and there, he started kicking him. Tom fell back and picked up a stick that was close by and hit Boo Boo right in his privates. And Tom was bout to hit him again before Kim pulled his fist back.

Boo Boo jumped to his feet and looked at Kim, Kim nodded. This was a sign that everything was okay. Boo Boo was about to asked Kim why Tom was there, but he dismissed it because Kim was his aunt and she never would do anything to harm him. Tom pulled out the extra food and clothes he had gathered for him and his family, in this big long coat. This triggered Boo Boo's mind to think way back about twenty years ago, he had stayed out with a black slave who was supposed to be in their quarters and not on the road. Tom had come along in the master carriage in the nick of time.

The bounty hunters were looking for Harriet Tubman. They ran up on him coming from the plantation, where his soon to be mate resided in. Boo Boo didn't have his papers. The bounty hunter had already selected a nice tree to lynch him. When Tom came up, he jumped off his carriage and walked the men a couple of steps down the road. What he said to them he didn't know. Boo Boo despised Tom. He thought Tom was probably telling something on him. Tom looked back with a sly smile on his face, then the bounty hunter told Boo Boo, "Come here Boy!" "This is your day, Next time there's gonna be a lynching. Go, Tom will take you back to Massa Pee's plantation."

Boo Boo jumped into the carriage but not before getting slapped by Tom. Tom drove off driving like a crazy man back to the plantation. Nothing was said. While Boo Boo was nursing his wounds, Tom looked at him with distaste. Boo Boo thought back to all the times Tom came in the nick of time and rescued him. Tom wasn't really who he portrayed himself to be. Tom made sure Boo Boo had what he needed for the travel. Tom also made sure that Boo Boo had a little moon shine to lighten his burden. "Ah, Tom thought, that boy gonna get tore up." Boo Boo ran that night. He thought about all the other slaves that were brave enough to venture out and run to the unknown. To a place where men were free. He had been bound and chained too long.

How Long Is Too Long! He needed to leave before the overseer discovered he was gone. Boo Boo hated Tom for so long. This man was another sell out, or was he? Didn't these sell-outs know they were still slaves?

William regretted not helping Boo Boo. He had denied the truth for so long. Now, he understood. The master gave him a title to make him think he had some sort of authority. This caused him to become big headed. How had he been so foolish to think that Massa would protect him, how could he be so blind? He was a slave; his rights were stripped from him the minute he set foot on American soil. He couldn't understand this and he refused to accept it.

Blue's mother Priscilla died at a young age, she was in her thirties.

The story would be passed down for generations.

Little William's step father tried to toughen him up by teaching him not to expose his feelings on his face. First, he told his son never grin in front of the white man and he should always look downward when talking to any white man. William Sr. knew that Massa Pee's brother was Little William's father but never brought it up. He taught William that protecting himself against the white man's rage, wasn't a sign of being a coward. It protected him from being perceived as a threat, a disrespected slave and any act of defiance resulted in death. Poor little William was instructed on how he should talk and told him that he needed to run when the Massa called. This made the Massa think he was superior to this black **slave thinking that** he has another Uncle Tom.

All these memories came back to William as he relived his childhood, on Massa' Pee Plantation.

William's father told him to bite his lip after talking to the Massa to harden his heart. William remembered all this after witnessing his woman being raped, and now, he had finally got what the old slaves were trying to tell him, Son, you are nobody in the white man eyes."

Now his mind had been restored, he was ready to fight no matter what it took or how hard the battle, he would become what the run-away slaves whispered in the late hours of the night, a run-away slave. He would risk his life to help save others. For months, William pretended to be passive while plotting his revenge. He would become one of those unsung heroes, a person willing to die and had the passion to survive until freedom rang far and wide.

Now, let's get back to Blue, he was enjoying the fruit of deception. After all, his father was

Captain Pee. Blue never used this to reap benefits, he knew his father had the money and power to protect him but would that be enough?

Priscilla

Blue's mother had died at an early age, she was only thirty-eight. Her name was Priscilla; his mother was one of the beautiful dark colored slaves Massa's Pee had on his plantation, and was the target of his wife's anger. Massa Pee's wife tormented Priscilla because she was the most favorite of all the slaves that her husband had slept with. He didn't even want to share a bed with her anymore. It was always this little witch that he slipped in and out of the bed every night. Why! Priscilla's skin tone was black like a mare in the summer months, but in the winter, her skin was light brown. Her hair was wooly, Priscilla had a face like a carved-out angel. She was breathtaking! All the white men that came to Massa Pee's plantation wanted her. Massa told them that she was his. He let them know if anyone touched her, the grave would be calling their name. But poor Priscilla lacked the mental capacity to raise poor Blue so his grandparents stepped in.

Blue's mother had been raped by Massa Pee. It happened when his mother was only thirteen years old. While Priscilla was in the woods one day chasing butterflies, the Massa told young Priscilla to come, he had a little butterfly and since poor Priscilla didn't understand, she hopped over to Massa Pee. Priscilla reached for the butterfly and that's when Massa Pee proceeded to rape her. She released the butterfly he had gave her and fell down on the leaves while he mounted himself and rode this poor girl like a horse. Priscilla screamed and screamed scratching him with her fingernails. She dug into the Massa's chest. This seemed to excite the Massa, he got so excited he pee on himself. The more she struggled, the more the Master roughed her up pounding on her flesh like a blacksmith hammering his tools. After it was over, Priscilla laid in her blood pouring from her legs. Her flesh was bruised, but what was that coming from between her legs? Blood was coming from everywhere. She ran and jumped in the river where she scrubbed and scrubbed, but the blood wouldn't stop coming. She started yelling and yelling. The Massa thought to himself another baby, he collected his clothing and wiped the sweat off his brow. Boy this was good, he thought to himself. When Priscilla came out of the water, she had a weird look on her face. She lunged at Massa Pee, running with a giant rock she had picked up by the river bed. The Massa wasn't having it, he wrestled her down and slapped her a couple of times before grabbing poor Priscilla and placing her on his back and carried her back to the ragged shack giving her to her mother. The mother nursed crying Priscilla and rubbed her hand on Priscilla's body, crying and looking up helplessly. Massa smiled, this truly was the best piece of tail he had ever had, and he was planning on taking her as often as he wanted. After all, "she was his slave, and she had no rights. Priscilla cried and cried; she didn't know that Massa had just made her period come on. Massa Pee had been admiring Priscilla for days. She was the most beautiful young slave he had ever come across and the fact that she lived on his plantation excited him even more. He had to have her. Property is Property. He couldn't resist the compelling feeling of her body next to his. He knew that Priscilla had a mind of a young child, but this was not his concern. His desires were all that mattered.

Massa Pee and Priscilla the slave girl
Kim helped when Priscilla gave birth to Blue.

Massa Pee had forced himself on this young slave girl. Forcing her to endure the pain that her young fragile body had ever experienced. After all, she was a virgin a person not touched by a man. From that day on, Massa came every night and continued his ritual of forcing this young girl to experience all kind of things, fetishes, and any sexual acts his depraved mind thought of. Never mind the fact that she held on to her rag dolls or laughed at the bright red bumps on his rear end. All Massa Pee cared about was this was fresh meat and he wanted the firstborn to be his. He didn't care if this slave girl had the mind of a two-year-old. He didn't care what it had to do with, his only concern was his manhood. All he could think about was, another new born to work the fields. Where was Priscilla's parents? Well, they knew but what could they do, the Massa controlled everything. From the time they got up in the morning, until the time they went to sleep at night. Priscilla's mother, nursed her bloody body, cleaning Priscilla up after every brutal rape.

After six months of the Massa sexing Priscilla up, she became pregnant, poor thing, she kept on playing with her rag dolls and catching her butter flies. When Priscilla went into labor, she hollered so loud, she woke up all that was in the Massa's house. Priscilla's mother sent for Kim, because Kim was the midwife for all the slaves. This was her duty, and she did a good job. Kim came, but so did Massa Pee. He came stuttering, half asleep. Yeah, Massa Pee came; he wanted to see if the baby was ripe or not worth his efforts. He hoped it would be a male child. Another slave he created to work the fields. Kim yelled out, it's a boy. Massa Pee couldn't contain himself. Ha, ha, ha, ha, ha, he took the boy and told Kim to clean the baby up and bring him to the main quarters. There, he would be raised by

Kim. He had all the pleasure of the plantation until he become of age. Then he would have to pay for his keeps. "Another boy." Massa Pee said. "Ha, ha." Blue, Priscilla's son was growing up, the more he became of age, the more he looked like Massa Pee. Larry, Massa Pee's oldest son didn't like the attention his father gave to Blue. He tried his best to sabotage Blue every chance he got. He planted stuff in Blue's room, but Kim watched and reported back to her master.

Every year, Mass Pee would go overseas to buy delectable items for his wife and some fancy things for himself. Lester, an old slave that taught the scriptures

Larry was Blue's brother. Larry had a younger brother, Kelly. Larry plotted to do away with Blue and his mom because he hated Blue. Priscilla dies at thirty- eight.

There was always someone willing to protect Blue, usually it was the old slave grandpa Lester that preached in his shack, being that he was secretly taught by his grandfather before him. It was Lester who alerted Massa Pee when Blue was in danger. This angered Larry.

Meanwhile, Blue continued to grow, and the more he grew, the more he became a spitting image of Massa Pee. This infuriated Larry and his mother. Larry's mom had demeaned Blue's mom, even though she knew this black slave wasn't aware she was being taunted or abused. If only she could touch Blue, she would blow his little black head off. Every opportunity Larry and his mother got, they tried to get Blue. Blue was the favorite. On several occasions, Larry and his mom tried to get Massa Pee to sell Blue. It was a bad idea. This pushed Massa Pee over the deep end. He told his wife and his son Larry, "If y'all say this again, I gonna blow both of y'all heads off!!" On this plantation, "Even the Massa couldn't understand his connection, the feeling he had for Blue. Nevertheless, Larry thought to himself, father will not be able to protect Blue forever, especially if I strike now! The fury of my father would surely cause me harm. This is a risk I can't take. But one day, he would make his move and get rid of Blue.

Blue was the best field hand on the plantation, but what did he care. The poison of envy had embedded in Larry and took up root.

Meanwhile, Blue continued to grow into a striking man. This made Larry hate him more. Blue couldn't understand why Larry hated him so much. But he was a slave.

But one night, when Massa Pee had gone overseas, he left Larry, his oldest son to run the planation. Larry had gone to buy more slaves in

Virginia. Sapphire, his wife decided it was her perfect opportunity to sample the forbidden fruit she wanted Blue. She knew by the way Blue looked at her that he wanted her also.

On that night while Blue and William were feeding the horses, Sapphire came to the stable. This time her eyes locked on Blue. Blue couldn't deny his craving for her any longer. He led Sapphire back to the woods. They had to have each other until they exhausted the fire that ran through their veins. After that night, Sapphire waited until Larry went to sleep after drinking the corn liquor that she had spiked with a crushed remedy to knock him out until she finished her escapade with Blue.

Little did Blue know, that he was dipping his hand in a pot and there would be no turning back. It was about to sizzle with hot flames. Sapphire had given him something that Little Millie couldn't. It was the touch of her soft white skin.

**Babies Born/ Hiring of
White Laborers for
Birthing Purposes**

Back in the good old days, as the privileged called it, poor whites were hired to work the plantation. It was the lady of the plantation whose task was to find suitable white laborers. But it became a sinister plot to find young white women to give birth to children for the pleasure of the lady of the house. Especially, if she was dipping in the pot, sleeping with the black slaves that was considered property of the Massa. It was well known why white cheap laborers were hired by the Massa's wife. It was to cover her infidelities that resulted in the Massa's wife birthing a child by a field slave or house slave. It seems kind of crazy, doesn't it?

These white laborers were groomed and treated very special. Sometimes, the mistress of the plantation showered them with the finest perfumed oils and schooled them on what to expect before the birth of the Massa's child, which usually occurred around the same time as their expecting child. Then the midwife, who was usually black, would escort the poor white laborers in one of the slaves' cabins. She waited until they got the sign that the Massa's wife was going into labor. And if there were any signs that the child wasn't the Massa's, the baby would be hurried in the arms of the midwife and taken to the back quarters immediately into the arms of a waiting slave. The timing had to be just right. Women having babies the same time was hard, but usually the midwives were very experienced and usually it went off without any complications. If there were any problems the midwives had another plan. She would claim the baby was born dead due to a disease the baby had. The child had to be buried right away because of a rare and contagious disease.

The mistresses and their secrets, having babies, surrogate poor white trash, birthing the mistress's child, because the child was born, evidently signs of the slave laborer's

offspring. This practice started way back. But the secret kept penetrating over the years.

Big secret, poor white laborer, all lies that were used to protect the white blood line. All done to hide the secret of betrayal.

Some of the white madams had liaisons with the young muscular black men and they had children that were passed off as the slaves. Who would dare have a child by a slave? It is unknown as to how it began, but most of the white women hid this from their mates until they got caught, and then all hell broke loose even though the Massa was busy doing his thing. Having sex with any of the slave women he chose but not his madam. The pure white Madame of the plantation was his darling. Oh no! If the Madame got caught, all she had to do was scream rape and it worked all the time. The Massa went into a rage and a lynched whomever she accused of rape.

Most of these unscrupulous ladies were used to getting what they wanted never mind it was a slave. All they cared about was their cravings. To have a young slave against their body, especially when they were well in their prime. These fashionable ladies lusted for what their husbands couldn't give them, especially since most of their husbands needed to go on extended trips to buy more slaves. They needed someone to satisfy their appetite.

Lady Pee remembered her mom and seeing her with a young buck half her age but she never voiced it to her father. Lady Pee knew this was taboo. Oh no, she loved her mother despite her having guilty pleasures. These upscaled plantation madams kept their guilty pleasures hidden. They hired poor white trash as surrogate when they made a boo boo. In other words, when they got pregnant by a black slave. To protect themselves from getting killed by their mates, the white madams of the plantation enlisted one of their trusted maidens, the trusted maiden was the one they confided in and she was the one that carried out the task of concealing the identity of the child's father until the maid was sure without any doubt the baby's skin color was white as snow.

It was no accident that they selected white field hands closer to their skin tone and their features. All because these women couldn't keep their hands and minds off the black slave men. This resulted in these madams having children deemed black because they contained a drop of slave blood. And to cover up their actions, the surrogate was there when the baby was born. If the baby had any signs of being black, they were given to a young black couple to raise as their own.

Josie, Grand Madame, the Matriarch, was Massa Pee's, mother, she had a man slave named Waymond,

Waymond was the Grand Madame's man slave. The Grand Madame kept him for her guilty pleasures. One time she made the biggest mistake, she got pregnant by Waymond. The baby came out jet black. But before the child could be slapped on his butt and breathe, she had the midwife take the poor baby to one of the quarters before her husband came. She told her husband the baby had died at birth. But in actuality, the child grew up thinking Waymond's mother was his mother instead of his grandmother. And the old folks kept it that way. The secret was hidden away, possibly forever. The child actually was Massa Pee's half-brother. This was a well-kept secret in the South. A lot of the madams used some of their selected slaves for entertainment and some of the slaves even fathered their children.

Most of these madams dressed gracefully. They had gatherings at their homes displaying their magnificent masterpieces. The furniture and fixtures were made for royalty. The women joked amongst themselves about the size of their slaves' private parts and talked about how they all had close calls. They almost got caught but they were rescued by the kitchen maiden or house slave when the Massa came home unexpectedly from his trip.

Grand Madame always had plenty of stories about her encounters and the younger women looked on admirably. She schooled the younger mistresses on everything. From pleasing their man, to ordering planation equipment, how to dress and what to do when a slave woman became defiant. Grand Lion, Massa Pee's wife was sharp also, she had an answer for everything. Even the older women couldn't compete with her. She had a beauty that embodied her existence. Many tried to grandstand her, but after a planned confrontation in the middle of the night, these rebels got their tails whipped. No defiance was met and the resistance was crushed.

Grand Madame had got old, and a new fresh blood was about to take the reign. Sure, Massa

Pee's wife thought she was going to be the next Grand Madame but, there was another just as hard as the monarch, and it was Sapphire. She was very beautiful. Sapphire was defiant, and she did whatever it took to get what she wanted. She had come from a family that had nothing but money.

Nevertheless, Sapphire was catching the Grand Lion's eye because she had all the things that the Grand Lion once possessed, beauty and control. But Sapphire couldn't control her urges, this was about to get her in hot water. Sapphire starts to neglect her wifely duties. Grand Lion had to watch Sapphire. She didn't know why, but something about this fancy lady disturbed her, and she had a good sense that something was about to happen.

But for now, the Grand White Party was all she focused on. She had to go shopping to make another grand entrance.

The Grand Lion was not called the Grand Lion for nothing, *she chewed up people and spit them out like chewing tobacco. She was just like the Grand Madame; she was hard core mean.*

When Massa Pee's mother, the Grand Madame, was young, she summoned Waymond from his chores to satisfy her every need; he was the Grand Madame's heart. He was her slave for whatever she wanted done to her. Waymond fulfilled all her dreams. Oh my, Grand Madame would wet her lips just thinking about him she could still taste the scent of this black slave. But now, she had only memories and her lips now were wrinkled with lines. The Grand Madame didn't care the least what anyone thought of her; she had lived her life. Although she should have been afraid, she had so much power. Her husband had almost caught her, but pride made him look the other way. He loved Grand Madame and that would be a hard pill to swallow every day. He was broken because he didn't like the fact she was sleeping with a slave. Over the years, he swallowed his pride and looked the other way. But he plotted to catch that no count bastard and that would be the end of that.

Little did he know that low down dirty bastard was his prize possession, the one who said, "yes sir Massa" the one who was the most reliable slaves on the whole plantation, Waymond. The more Massa thought, maybe he could enlist Waymond to help him find that low down dirty bastard, and a lynching was due for touching his possession, his lady known as the Grand Madame. If she demanded it, it was hers, if she hated it, it was destroyed, and if she couldn't have it, then no one would. It would disappear without a trace. Even though she had

destroyed her husband's pride, he couldn't do anything to her; her family was the wealthiest family in the entire country and the wrath of what would happen to him if he did anything to this slave lover would have a diehard effect. Sure, the Massa had power, but nothing compared to her family, and he knew that it would end badly for
him if he touched a hair on the Grand Madame's head. Even if she did the unthinkable, her father's wrath would have no boundaries.

One of Grand Madame's sisters was caught with a slave and her husband berated her in front of the neighboring plantation. Days later, he was found hanging from a tree and his wife was shipped overseas. The body of her husband hung for days without anyone claiming the body. Now, you see why Massa Pee was cold; his mother, the Grand Madame was cold as ice.

Sapphire couldn't stop her urges to see Blue every chance she got, especially when Sapphire's husband went away to purchase more slaves at the market in Mississippi, Sapphire had a run of the whole plantation. Now Sapphire could see Blue in her quarters, and boy she did. They demolished the bedroom in their heated sexual acts. So, it wasn't a surprise when Sapphire started having morning sickness after missing several periods. Some might ask, why didn't

Massa Pee and Lady Pee hear all the wild love making, well, no they didn't because Larry and Sapphire's quarters were separate from the main quarters in the mansion, and their quarters

were spectacular; it was even as grand as the big house.

Sapphire had taken precautions if she was to get pregnant, she had hired a surrogate, a white laborer who had no family. The white laborer had her own private quarters on the property. The poor laborer was hired to get pregnant the same time, and produce a child when the madam of the house was due. No word of this deception or there would be diehard consequences, even death. The laborers knew not to tell, after all, she had all the luxuries that the madam had, and in return, she just had to pledge secrecy to the cause. And being poor, this opportunity of getting anything you wanted was too much to pass up. What happened if she refused, she heard the rumors? Some of the stories she had heard, were terrifying; stories of white women being found on the riverbanks or the woods dead and insects feeding on their remains.

Blue and Sapphire love
Blue and Sapphire/firstborn

The firstborn was snow white with no features displaying any signs of Blue being his father. It could have been her mate but, her dates didn't calculate with the time the baby was born. Plus, she could always lie and he would believe anything she said. Sapphire raised the baby as her husband's child. And boy, her husband loved him.

He took the young boy every place he went. And when the boy got older, he took him on fishing trips. He also let the young child ride in the field and inspect the work done by the slaves. His skin coloring never changed, if anything he got lighter. He had the most beautiful hazel eyes. But Larry and Sapphire noticed the stares, and the slave women nodding amongst themselves. No, he was so into his baby boy.

Sapphire showered her baby with all her affections. She didn't even allow the nurse that was accustomed to breastfeeding their master's child to breastfeed him. Sapphire did this herself.

Blue knew that this was his baby, he got sick when Sapphire was experiencing her morning sickness. The old women shook their head. Another black slave stuck in a triangle with the Massa's family.

He would come when the Massa was gone on his trip and play with the youth as much as he could because he knew when the youth became of age, he would not be able to see him fearing it would get back to Sapphire's husband. It was a shame, that he couldn't openly acknowledge his own son, but it was a price he was willing to pay to protect the welfare of his son.

Nevertheless, Blue was getting tired; he wanted a stable life with one of his own. And he knew the right one, she had just been sold to Massa Pee and she was beautiful. Blue had talked to her on several occasions trying to get her to notice him, but she didn't seem interested. He wondered why?

But Sapphire had noticed the look that Blue gave her when he came around. She had to talk to this slave and explain what was what. Blue knew nothing about this. Finally, a house maiden told him the dirt. Blue couldn't approach Sapphire because he knew what she would do firsthand if she couldn't have her way. So, he continued appeasing her every need, but he was falling for this black creature, whose skin was darker than midnight. What was a man to do? He had a baby by this woman. He was tied down with different kind of chains. But somehow, he had to find a way to get his son. Somehow, he had to go and find his way to freedom, where he was a man and not a slave

Blue had taken a shining to a slave girl named, Josephine, Millie was the white laborer

Blue loved Sapphire but he got tired of her demanding ways and took a shining to a slave

**woman name Millie and the poor white
laborer and Sapphire's baby boy**

Sapphire had gotten bold, she demanded Blue's attention every chance she got. She had dodged the bullet this time because her baby boy looked white. Sapphire had no need for Millie's son now, she could now raise her own son and pass him off as Massa Larry's child. Never mind, the rolled eyes from the house slaves or the secret whispers that ended when she entered the quarters, these slaves couldn't touch her! She was white. Blue was her buck and no slave better touch him, y' all hear me! Money, power and her family ruled the south. Who dare touch him! Ha, ha!

Poor Blue, he really liked the new slave, named Josephine. He loved Sapphire, but he loved Josephine equally. If he refused Sapphire, he knew what would happen. He witnessed it firsthand when he came home from working in the fields and saw Sapphire beating Josephine. What could he do? She was Massa Larry's wife. There wouldn't be any boundaries to her fury. If he had only listened to William, he wouldn't be in this mess. But how could he keep up with Sapphire's demanding appetite and please Josephine too?

What was he to do? Especially, since Sapphire was with child again. Blue trembled. How did he get into this mess?

{Chapter two} The Reckoning

The bounty hunter slapped Sapphire around and Massa Pee burst into the room, no signs of Blue

The night of the Annual White Ball, Sapphire seemed in extremely good spirits. She admired the creature that reflected back from her mirror. Then she heard a strange noise. Without knocking, the bounty hunters stormed into her room. She had on a beautiful lace gown with layers of fabric and had a pink bow on her newly braided hair. "What's this?" She yelled. Where's the slave called, Blue? Sapphire couldn't help herself, she replied, "how would I know where a slave is at"? 'He is probably in his ragged shack."

The men walked around looking at her with disgusting looks, one yelled out, if we could touch you, we would hang you because your power ranks high. Ha, ha, but we can touch the bastard you have been sleeping with and when we get him, he is as good as lynched.

Sapphire fell back, she finally got it. She had become so self-absorbed that she didn't realize she was putting Blue at the mercy of a lynching.

She had to think fast. How could she protect Blue and not expose herself? But before she could think of a good bold face lie, the bounty hunters were searching every corner and every crack, looking for Blue, under her bed, in her closet; they were searching everywhere. While they searched the plantation, another group went to Blue's shack. In his quarter was a big bowl of water, with rags, like someone was about to take a wash up. But there were no signs of Blue, the men went running back to the plantation.

After the bounty hunters didn't find any sign of Blue, they marched back to the plantation. "Where is Blue", the main bounty hunter asked Sapphire again? One of the bounty hunters had already slapped Sapphire around when Massa Pee burst into the room, and Massa Pee was bad.

Massa Pee and sweet Maylene, they were lovers, even though, they both was married.

The Reckoning? Who will pay? Sapphire or Blue

When Massa Pee got word of a lynching and his pride possession, Blue was about to be lynched, he flew into a rage beating his chest.

At the White Ball, he was enjoying the taste of Maylene's fruits, after he excused himself and found his way to sweet Maylene's parlor. Maylene was a little hefty, but she was very stunning. It never bothered her that Massa Pee was married. Hell, she was too. But it was something that kept him constantly going back, and she never refuse him. Massa Pee loved the way Maylene smelled. Her body felt like soft feathers.

Massa Pee sowed his oats everywhere and it was rumored that he had fathered Maylene's oldest child, but it was never mentioned around Massa Pee.

Lady Pee, The Grand Lion was downstairs chattering away with a crowd of young women who were excited to see just what she was wearing. They knew Lady Pee knew the latest gossip, because Lady Pee knew all the latest dirt on everyone.

She was dressed in a rosy pink dress that fitted her shape and highlighted her best attributes, her buttocks.

After Massa Pee finished enjoying the company of sweet Maylene, he pulled out his cigar and smoked; awe, Maylene knew how to please a man.

Maylene sat back on the bed; she was exhausted because Massa Pee had the energy of a young buck. Massa Pee noticed something different about Maylene's demeanor, instead of the jolly Maylene, she had a concerned look on her face. He quickly dismissed it and rolled over for round two of their love making.

After they finished, Maylene, grabbed him and said, "Pee you know I care about you, don't you?" 'Yes, Maylene, please don't start crying again, "you know this can't ever be," he said. Maylene took a deep breath, Pee they're gone up to your plantation and they're going to lynch Blue. Massa Pee looked at Maylene. He knew she would never lie to him. If he told her to leave her husband and come with him, Maylene would throw all her things together and leave right then and there. She loved him and the only reason she got married to her no count husband was because Massa Pee had married Lady Pee. Lady Pee came from one of the richest families in the South.

Maylene handed Massa Pee his trousers. He rushed to put them on and gave her a hug. Maybe, I should have married Maylene, he thought to himself. She has more class than that piece of white trash he had married. All Lady Pee wanted to do was shop overseas.

Wow, can you believe this? Massa Pee calling someone white trash. Such a dirty low-down scandal. Man, just pull up your pants. He rushed downstairs, he saw the puzzled look on the people faces and saw his wife turn around and was about to ask where was he going? But before she could, he yelled back at Lady Pee "stay here!"

"I gotta go, one of my slaves will bring a carriage and escort you home." She was bout to say something but he had gone that fast.

The White Ball was the time that all the super-rich slave plantation owners got together and celebrated their crops coming in and talked about their slaves. Sometimes they argued about who had the most slaves and how rich they were.

Let me get back to Massa Pee, he was so mad, he started to shot somebody right then and there. If Marlene hadn't stopped him, he would have put a bullet in the white waiter that almost burst in the room after Marlene disclosed to him what was going on. Death be it; it was the only way the other plantation owners would have a chance to touch even a hair on Blue's Head.

Massa Pee had a younger son, his name was Kelly. He was the spitting image of Blue but with an ivory complexion. Blue was light brown. Kelly had blue eyes; this fella was gorgeous. Massa Pee had sent Kelly to the best school abroad, and Kelly had done well for himself. But Massa Pee couldn't get a good read as to what Kelly was thinking because he always seemed angry. But I'll get back to Kelly later. Because unbeknownst to everyone, Kelly had a secret.

Now, back to Boo Boo, he had given one of Massa Pee's horses some poison and killed it. Massa Pee named another horse Midnight.

Massa Pee rode Black Midnight Madness hard; Midnight Madness was called Madness because no one could ride this horse but Massa Pee, not even the slaves. I guess the horse had gotten used to Massa Pee, farting and it smelled good to the horse. Midnight started panting hard, but Massa continued to ride, he couldn't stop for a moment, Blue's life depended on him.

Getting back to Kelly, Kelly had a secret only his mother knew; Kelly worked hard alongside the slaves, when he came back from overseas, he worked the fields as hard as any slave but it seemed to everyone but his mother, he was a little too tough on them. Kelly knew everything that happen on the plantation and the slaves thought, he was hard core nasty.

But unbeknownst to them, it was only an act. If the slaves knew the truth, Kelly's life would be in jeopardy, because there were several Uncle Toms on the plantation that were more than willing to tell. He had to be very careful. He carried on this charade, to protect himself as well as the slaves who sought to escape to the Underground Railroad. Most of the slaves thought he was bad-mannered; but oh no, he had so much compassion, he cried thinking about how any man could subject people to such inhumane treatments. This hurt Kelly and this made him become more active in his quest to help the slaves become free souls.

Kelly was one of the main contributors of the Underground Railroad, he sent money from abroad to help finance its existence. He hated the way slaves were treated. He couldn't understand why the white men and women, enjoy stripping people pride away for them. Buying, selling human beings and treating them like property while beating and humiliating them, this to him was very inhumane. But he hid his feelings for the better cause.

Massa Pee didn't even have a clue that Kelly was against slavery; In Kelly mind, slavery represented evilness and the reason it existed so long was unimaginable to him. His mother knew about Kelly feelings but kept his secret, after all, he was her baby. She protected him because she knew if it was revealed, it would have a damning affect, and could result in her son demise.

Oh, Kelly had heard about the infidelities of Blue with Sapphire, he wanted to act, but he was powerless because if the other slave owners knew he disagreed with the way slaves was treated, they would lose trust and deem him a threat. Blue was in trouble, but he had someone least expected that was willing to die alongside him, his half-brother, Kelly.

A group of plantation owners and bounty hunters were on their route to The Bronze Plantation. They had ridden hard.

Because they wanted to get, this lynching done before Massa Pee returned from the White Ball.

They had disturbed Sapphire's plans; she had already taken a good bath and perfumed her body down. Now she was waiting for Blue, just waiting like she did midnight every Sunday, she was looking forward to a wild night.

But Kelly had somehow gotten news of what were about to happen that there were going be a lynching and the target was Blue, he rode his horse with hast. If he didn't reach Blue in time, Blue's body would be hanging from a tree. He was only a few miles away; he had been out running some errands for his father. He reached the plantation, and noticed some strange horses in the stable so, he sneaked around to the shack that Blue occupied. Massa Pee had just purchased two white horses. But Kelly thought, it was the bounty hunters out to get Blue. Kelly looked into the clean shack, it looked like Blue was bout to wash up, he grabbed him by the neck, this startled Blue because not once did

Kelly ever acknowledged his presence. "Let's go Blue!" Kelly ordered. Blue looked confused but without giving it another thought, Blue jumped into the wagon, and Kelly whipped the horses knocking down, everything in his path. The bounty hunters and plantation owners were just a few minutes away before they stormed the planation. Blue didn't know what was going on, but remained silent, because he knew that it must be mighty bad for Kelly to do this. Especially since Kelly was so mean and treated him like a disease.

Kelly ordered Blue to change clothes in the wagon, while he continued to whip the horse's full speed. Blue did as Kelly asked. Then, Kelly told Blue that he had gotten words that the bounty hunters were coming to lynch him and he heard the order had come from Sapphire's father. Sapphire didn't know her father had found out about her infidelities and the babies she and Blue had produced together. Sapphire's father got so mad, he vowed to kill the dirty black bastard. A black slave touching his pride and joy, this required death. Sapphire's father would have killed Blue himself but he was to fat, to take the long trip. Plus, he knew Massa Pee would skin him alive if he came close to

Blue on his plantation. That is why Sapphire's father enlisted the help of the bounty hunters and he knew the perfect opportunity to strike like a snake, Awe, the night of the White Ball. Sapphire's father knew that Massa Pee would be enjoying himself, because he never missed the opportunity to brag and talk about what he had acquired. That why he chose that night. Sapphire's father, laughed, that black bastard will not know what hit him. Kelly told Blue, they had to make ground fast before dawn catch them or they both would surely get lynched. Blue did everything that Kelly asked of him.

After almost an hour, Kelly dropped him off to an inn surrounding by woods. Blue had seen this inn before but not in the dark of the night.

Kelly told him to say to the inn keeper, "peace be with your friend" and they will open the door.

Sapphire is killed by bounty hunter

The bounty hunters looked afraid. Massa Pee had just stormed in the room, and he was red. They knew Massa Pee was one of the strongest men in the whole county, because when someone tried to take what was his, they were met with a beat down, fist or gun it didn't matter to him. Massa Pee had fought the best and strongest slaves and was rumored to have the strength of ten men. This man had so much money, that he had to ship some of it overseas to banks to accommodate his vast fortune. There were only a few Plantations that could equal his worth. The Brown Plantation owner, deep in the southern woods and the Sugar Plantation located in Mississippi. But let get back to the bounty hunters. How were they going explain this intrusion on Massa Pee's property?

Sapphire started laughing but, little did she know, Massa Pee had heard the rumors and knew that they were true. Sapphire had gone too far this time. She started prancing around the room. This made one of the bounty hunters so angry he forgot she was a white lady. He couldn't contain his distaste for her because he seen this white woman eyeing the black slaves. Lusting after a slave was unacceptable in his eyes. And without thinking about the consequences, he pointed his pistol straight toward her face and pulled the trigger, blowing her fragile body fifteen feet away. She was a slave lover." He could not stand for that. A slave sympathizer was worse than a slave. She was one of the worse of the worse. The bounty hunter in a fit of rage, had shot and killed Massa Pee's daughter-in-law. After regaining his senses, he started pleading with Massa Pee to spare his life.

The bounty hunter started making excuses, saying it was an accident. The rage had built up in Massa Pee; he took his pistol and pistol whipped him before he shot a single bullet in middle of his heart killing him dead. Oh, yes! Someone had to pay for coming to his plantation and disturbing its flow. They had to pay for this intrusion. Massa Pee pointed his gun and shot a second time, shooting the man's head off. Then he ordered his men to shoot, while he battled the ring leader, fist to fist. Knocking down furniture, breaking down beds while finally, he overpowered the scrawny looking man. Massa Pee glanced at the body of Sapphire. She was dead. Even though he didn't like her, someone had to pay for her untimely death. He shot two more bounty hunters, hitting one in the arm, then he shot the other straight in the back. The others backed up, but Massa Pee, said "either you signed this paper stating you came on my property without cause or I will shoot you dead". The other bounty hunters signed the notes to that effect. "Never voice what happened here on this day, if you tell anyone I will hunt you down, and there will not be a resting place for you to hide from my rage." He asked one of the surviving bounty hunters, "Why did he come to his plantation?" The man shaking, nervously said, "to kill your slave Blue." "Blue is my slave; he is my property. In a rage Massa Pee, shot the bounty hunter dead.

The other bounty hunters, told Massa Pee that they were paid a ransom by Sapphire's father to Kill Blue. Massa Pee hit the table; retribution is mines. He will get his when he finds out his daughter has been killed because of him. He will seek to take what I own but, we will see who has the upper hands. Massa Pee went into a rage, yelling at his men to kill them of all! One of the bounty hunters, jumped through the big glass window, but a bullet hit him right between the

eyes. This meant and eye for an eye, who dare come on Massa Pee property and destroy something he worked hard to accomplish?

Massa Pee knew the first time he set eyes on Sapphire's father, there was something that troubled him about this stocky man.

What will happen when Sapphire's father finds out Sapphire was dead? The war between the powers would explode and who would survive? Who would be the victor or who will get crushed? But now, he had to find Blue.

Massa Pee stormed out of the plantation, and ran over to where Blue lived. When he entered the half-lit cabin, he noticed that a pan was on the table and it looked like Blue was bout to wash up. The fire was almost out. Where was Blue?

Now, let get back to William and his family, the time had finally arrived, William gathered his

family and made a run. But before he left, he had
to pay back Tom, the white laborer. Tom, the
white laborer was living on the neighboring
plantation ten miles from the Bronze Plantation.
Two slaves were recruited to help William get
Tom to the Plantation that night. They told Tom
that there was a slave girl whom never been
touched by a man. Tom couldn't help himself,
boy he was so excited. That night Tom, washed
his face but didn't let no water touch his private
part and he was known to have a bad odor. Tom
hurried to Massa Pee's plantation. He was ready
to shove his manhood into the young slave and
destroy what thoughts she had of transitioning
into womanhood. But the closer Tom got to
where the little girl was supposed to be, he
noticed the men looking down but at what?
Bring me the gal, Tom ordered! But before he
had a chance to turn around, William had
knocked him slam out. The two recruits and
William were throwing punches left and right,
when Tom turned one way, another man would
hit him; he was bounced back and forth. William
gave a single punch to the head and knocked
Tom slam out. Then William said, 'enough,
Let's take him in the woods. The three men
dragged Tom into the woods and starting beating
him some more. When Tom came through, he

yelled," What the hell are y'all doing". I'm a white man! And when he looked up and saw William, he started shaking. Tom knew then and there; it was retribution time. Tom scrambled to get up but William was too fast, William landed blow after blow knocking Tom back on the ground. Then the other two men held Tom down, while William got his ax. When Tom saw what was about to happen, he started kicking and fighting to save his manhood, but with one slice of the ax, it had been cut off and William was nursing it in his hand. "This is for touching me and mines, William said." Tom had raped poor Quinta and surely, he had to pay for that humiliation. This time William had chosen not to turn the other cheeks. Oh, no! Tom needed to pay; William had waited and waited for this opportunity, and now, it was time for retaliation.

Ha, ha, Tom cried out in pain, but William felt no remorse, he took his time cutting off the little thing, so Tom could feel the agony.

Tom fainted and when he woke up, he was alone in the woods with only the snakes and bears to comfort him. He put pressure on the wound to stop the bleeding then he stumbled back to his little cottage. After he picked up his manhood off the ground, he looked at it and hurried to put it on ice to save it. What would he do now, with no manhood, to rape and torment the young slave girls? Who just laid there like a ghost while he did what he wanted to do with her, the young slaves had to put a rag up her nose to seal the stench coming from Tom's body?

What about the men who helped William get his sweet revenge? Well, they packed up their stuff and high tailed it out of there. After all, they had enough. William left that night on his journey to taste freedom.

After the Civil War, William became skilled at building things, he became an inventor. He had invented things when he was a slave but Massa Pee proudly took the credit like so many other inventions that were stolen and given to white men for them to claim. William's wife became a teacher. Nevertheless, when William was a slave, he became well known for his knowledge and planted the seed of hope. He helped his fellow slaves by donating funds for their escape to safe houses.

He lived a full life and told stories about his life as a slave. William continued his quest to improve his family's life until he died.

What happened to Kelly and Blue? Kelly crammed Blue into a box and carried Blue on the ship with the help of two young hefty slaves. He told his friend who was the captain, that he was going on a trip to England and he was taking some things to sell. He boarded the ship with Blue in the box. Kelly had been careful to make sure Blue could breathe; he persuaded the captain to let him keep the big box in his quarter. There, he made sure Blue ate and got a proper bath. But before he left, he had gotten Blue's son to safety until he could make a path for his freedom. This was the second time that Kelly had rescued Blue. The last time was when Massa Pee, Kelly and Blue's father solicited him to rescue Blue from a hanging. This shocked Kelly, was his father finally changing his heart?

Kelly had already set up a place where Blue could blend in and make a home for himself. Kelly had traveled to England when he was young and was schooled by the best educators. And when he got older, he went back and established a striving business. Kelly realized if Blue was going to have any kind of life, he needed to live in a country that was more liberal than America.

Kelly's had a huge mansion in England. His father, Massa Pee knew about Kelly's wealth. Hell, Massa Pee was super rich himself. What happen to Blue after he established himself in a foreign country? Later on, Blue would use his skills to go back and get his lady, Josephine and his other son.

One of his oldest sons by Sapphire was already with him. Blue learned how to read effortlessly and became a teacher. He wrote several books detailing the slaves' struggles. He later told his son about his mother and how they had fell in love, a love not meant to be. He taught his son to cherish life and never forget the black man's struggles. This struggle that continued to be bathed in innocent blood even today. But Blue was ready when he heard that a Civil War was approaching. "Yes, I will go and fight for my fellow slaves," Blue said.

But for now, I will answer the question that is on everyone's mind, what Massa Pee did when he found out William and his family had run away. The next day after William's family ran away, Massa Pee got up, had his big breakfast that Kim cooked and like always, he went to inspect and tell William what he wanted him to do, but William was gone. When he went to the little shack, it was empty. He screamed and screamed! Massa Pee ran out the little hut screaming. "If I find that bastard, I'm gonna kill him. 'He's "My Property, My Property." Everyone on the plantation heard Massa Pee's screams, the slaves knew there was no end to Massa Pee's rage because his face was pale white. Lady Pee went into her room and hid; the slaves went in their quarters; they were afraid.

What was bout to happen now? Massa Pee was ready to lynch someone. Massa Pee ran and ran. He was already mad because the North wanted to end slavery and now his prize possession had done run off, someone had to pay! But who? The south, they were behind Massa Pee.

But for now, someone had to get lynch for that no count slave and his family running away but the question, who?

Slaves running away

Freedom

{Chapter Three}

Mr. Ed and his journey to manhood
Mr. Ed, a descendant of slaves.
Mr. Ed's story is a continuation of the sagas that the descendants of William faced in this story. Mr. Ed's story fast forwards to the 1900ths. There are different scenarios, but very much the same outcome we are facing today. Even though we are living in different times, racism still run like a plague engulfing anyone who comes into contact with this immoral wickedness called racism.

The second part of this book, Mr. Ed faced uphill battles that were rooted in hate long before he was born. This story invites you into the life of Mr. Ed, a person doomed to failure even though he fought a fight conquering some of his demons while holding on to others. Eventually, alcoholism would be his downfall.

Mr. Ed's life was exciting by all means. He struggled to overcome his destructive pleasures that caused a rift in his foundation.

Let's take a moment and look into Mr. Ed's past and present behavior to see why this man was doomed to fail. Fate helped him become a rare soul whether it was right or wrong, Mr. Ed lived his life the way he wanted.

Mr. Ed had a lot of children and he instilled in them some good and wholesome qualities. This would later be a foundation for his children to serve as a positive role model. This man worked hard despite his abuse of alcohol. For those of you that have dealt with a person that has substance abuse, you can relate to these truths. Hopefully, you too will find a remedy to reclaim your freedom from a path rooted in pain giving you the guts to fight back and create a life that will allow you to achieve the ultimate dream.

Mr. Ed's story is a story seen through the eyes of Josie and visualized only through the window of her soul. Josie shielded herself from the world around her by escaping reality and venturing off into a world of make-believe, a world filled with flowers, sunshine and creatures that were loving and pleasing to the eyes. This softened her blows and helped her become a creative thinker. This helped her to explore beauty with her writing, empowering her to become a poet and writer. She used her gift to fight back and not bow down, she plowed the road ahead full speed.

Oh, Little Ed, was feeling all the bumps, he was on the floor in his dad's car. His father was driving like he was crazy; He feared his dad might stop the car at any minute and turn around, this would mess up everything.   As his father continued on his journey, all of a sudden, he came across a shack in an isolated area that was situated deep in the woods. There was only a small shack that sat on a raggedy foundation. When Little Ed got closer, his eyes started burning, he had just stumbled on a goal mine that he only heard about from other kids, talking about the grown-up's palace, but now, his eyes were on the real deal. The shack had a juke box and only grown-ups were allowed to drink and indulge in all their guilty pleasures.

   Little Ed got closer as the music rang in his ear, inviting him to move and this little boy wobbled and wobbled all around the trees. Why this place was for grown-ups, little kids needed a place to jam too? Little Ed twisted and turned until his little fragile body collapsed on the ground.

   Then he noticed a familiar figure that pierced through the crowd, surrounded by ladies on both sides, when the figure got closer, he almost gave out a loud cry, It's Pop! What's he doing with those strange ladies? Then, Little Ed heard the juke joint light up. Pop. And everyone in that raggedy shack was doing the boogie lo, awe, the music had Little Ed moving those little legs; with music like that, he had to move. He rocked back

and forth with every beat. And from that day
forth, Little Ed was determined that he
would become as smooth as that cat in the black
hat that had on a pair of red shoes. Little did he
know the cat's name was Boogie. Every
Saturday, Little Ed would slip in the car waiting
because he knew his pop would pick a fight with
his mother, so he could go out with the boys into
a world filled of entertainment, booze and ladies.
But all Little Ed wanted to do was dance, after
watching Boogie, he knew he needed to learn all
he could from that cat.

William, Little Ed's dad

Boogie had the moves, he would jump
back and forth, jumping down on his feet and
rocking both legs like a rocking horse or
something. This sent the ladies screaming. This
was the attention Little Ed craved for. His daddy
had all the ladies. The ladies didn't know this
man tortured his family every day and well into
the middle of the night. But later for that, Little
Ed saw the most beautiful creature that the world
was only beholding.

There she was standing, by the juke joint,
with her beautiful dark-skin and she had the most
beautiful fiery red hair that Little Ed had ever
seen.

When she saw Mr. Ed, it was all over, she
walked like she was sliding elegantly over the

floor until her small frame got William's attention. Did she know Mr. Ed had tons of women? Mr. Ed turned around and welcomed this beautiful creature, dismissing the other ones he had wrapped around his arms. The other women didn't look shocked, they acted like this was normal. The little red hair lady walked over and winded herself in Mr. Ed's arms while he openly tasted the scents of her lips as he slid his tongue down her throat. She moved her body like a snake twisting and turning with every beat of the juke box. What was wrong with these women? How disgusting, Little Ed thought to himself. But the night was still young, and that cat named Boogie was on a roll.

But Little Ed was getting sleepy. He needed to get back home because his father looked like he was going to stay all night.

He slipped down from the broken window and started his journey back to his little quant house.

On the way home he thought about his mom, a nice home maker; but he couldn't understand why she put up with his father's abuse.

Little Ed had been bitten by the dancing bug; he practiced the moves he saw his father's friend doing until he perfected it. But he had to go back and learn more moves. Little Ed wanted to be just like Boogie, the show stopper. If he practiced enough, he would achieve his goal. So, every day, he practiced and practiced until he became so smooth on his feet that it looked like he was floating. He became famous for his moves, later on, he would be known as Superfly.

Overseer, Mr. Pa the white boss that had a lot of money and racist, but he liked black women

Little Ed continued following his father in the woods and watching that cat named Boogie dance like he was moving on air. He watched and watched until he got down all Boogie's moves.

If he continued to practice, when he grew up, he would be like Boogie and his father, have all the ladies. Awe, He smiled; this was what he longed for. So, every weekend, he would slip into his father's car and wait until his dad got out, then he would slip out by the window and watched and watched. He observed his daddy's moves trying to capture the essence of his purpose and why his charm incited the ladies.

One night, when Little Ed was sleeping in the car, he almost got caught by his daddy, but his daddy, stumbled back in the house, I guess to argue with Della because he just had to get the last word. Little Ed waited and waited, then he fell asleep. When he woke up, he was already at the shack. What time was it? Had he been sleeping a long time? He didn't even know it. He crawled out of the back seat, and headed toward his favorite spot, the broken window in the back. This time it seemed something was off, he noticed a white man there and the aura just didn't feel right, when he stared closer, he recognized the man as being the overseer Mr. Pa. Just when Little Ed thought something was about to happen, Mr. Pa, grabbed one of the black ladies and started dancing, he was hugging her so tight but it seemed she had experienced him doing this and she just hugged him and laughed like they were friends. After Mr. Pa finished, he ordered some drinks and told everyone to drink up. He stumbled with the black lady still on his arms, and headed for the back door of the shack. He didn't see Mr. Pa for a couples of hours. When he came back, he looked like he had wrestled with a bear, the nice lady looked like she had gotten into a fist fight, her hair was a mess with her clothes looking all untidy.

But where was Boogie? He saw a guy laying on a table, the guy was knocked out. I guessed he had too much corn liquor, poor man.

One-time Little Ed followed his dad to the shack. Some white people busted into the old

shack looking around, with their rifles in hand.
All hell was about to break loose. Mr. Ed was
 slow grinding with his favorite lady friend,
Teona. One of the white men yelled out,
has anyone seen Boogie? Everyone shook their
heads no, but the white men were not having it.
  They were about to tear the place up when Mr.
Pa came out from the back, the white men
looked afraid and they should have. Mr. Pa was
the head leader of the KKK. What the hell y'all
doing here? He asked. "One of the whites said,
"we looking for Boogie," you're late, said Mr.
Pa. I just hung that no count, so and so. Get the
hell off my property before I string one of you
up. Oh, no, Boogie is dead. How could you kill a
guy with moves like that? But no one seemed
disturbed. It was so odd. Little Ed waited and
waited. Before he left, he wanted to be sure there
were no white men around because he didn't
want to get lynched. Why was Boogie killed?
He would learn about the answer to this question
much later. But for now, he had to get back to
his little shack with all his hair on his head. And
he would never return to the place called the
"Hole in the Wall," a place to go where you
could forget for one moment that your black
behind was free to do what you wanted to do.
Free to dance, free to love, and free to be a man!

That's what my dad solely wanted. But now, he longed for his bed with a homemade quilt and bedding his mother had made, where he could rest after seeing the hateful look on the white men's faces looking to string Boogie up.

Mr. Ed had gotten so irritated. Why was Boogie lynched? What did he do to deserve getting himself lynched?

Finally, Little Ed was home. He could never risk going back for fear of those mean looking white men. Suppose they tried to lynch him, he was only half a man not grown up yet.

He jumped through the window, and tip toed to his bed, everyone was asleep, but his brother woke up, and turned over. Wow, it had been a close call he thought. In his bed, he thought about Boogie until he finally fell asleep.

Back to when Ed met Della

Little Ed, had finally grown up; he met a neighboring young lady, named Della and had fell in love with her. Della was a beautiful brown lady who had two children. He had known her for years and they had gotten close. His mother loved Della. Because Della was so special, even though she had some problems in the past dealing with her mental status

{Chapter Four}

**Mr. Ed caused Della to unleash
The Big Bad Wolf, what will
happen to their family?**

Mr. Ed, "The Big Bad Wolf
        The harder Little Ed tried do the right thing,
the more obstacles he had to face. His father,
William had passed down some of the family
traits hidden in the subconscious mind for years.
Secrets that Little Ed was destined to become the
model image of. Little Ed sometimes wondered
why the world denied him the opportunity of just
being a little boy. He worked doing grown-men
work when he was a little boy. The sharecropper
required it.
        One thing his father taught him was how to
be strong, even when the odds were against you.
Little Ed's father taught him to fight like his life
was at stake when he got pushed in a corner.
One of his best strategies depended on him
outsmarting his oppressor. This he learned at an
early age, how to outthink his oppressors before
they gained the upper hand; he did whatever it
took to be victorious at any cost.
Growing up, Little Ed was shy, he lacked the
confidence that his father had, but he had the
Look! Along with that, he also inherited the use

of his fist. People called him Superfly because he was so light on his feet and so fast, his opponents didn't know that they had got a blow to their head until they stumbled to the ground.

Mr. Ed inherited his father's skills. He came from a long line of artistic individuals that was gifted in so many ways. Mr. Ed's talent was rooted in his father's footsteps from an early age. Mr. Ed inherited his father's slim physique along with his magnetism and his sex appeal. He drew women to him like flies. He was sly but when he drank, he became Super fly, not afraid of anything.

Oh, Mr. Ed didn't mean to act conceited, but with so many young ladies throwing every piece of item at him, his head became gigantic. Not only did he have the Look, black as the midnight sky; he was built. And, he had teeth so white, they lit up. Oh, his voice was magnifying. It was so deep and mesmerizing. Mr. Ed was smaller than the rest of his father's children but, his swiftness prevented them from getting the best in the end. And when he threw a punch, they landed with precision.

William's mother and grandmother passed down the story to Little Ed's dad, William

Mr. Ed's dad was called William, and his dad before him was called William. William's mother and grandmother had passed down the story to him, William told his wife the story and when Little Ed got older, his mother passed the story down to him. The story detailed a period in slavery when Blacks were considered the white man's property and they were sold at their discretion. After hearing the story, some of William's descendants developed a deep-seated hate for all white people.

William's grandmother sat him down one day and began telling him the story. His mother had told him little bits and pieces but his grandmother got down to the nitty gritty. And this story has circulated down from decades.

When Little Ed grew up, he met Della and they married. They had a good life considering they still were not allowed comfort under the white man's rule. They still lived in a time where whites looked at Blacks as being inferior. So, when they addressed black men, they still called them boys insulting their intelligence. But life was good for Della and Ed, both had problems, Mr. Ed developed into a full pledged alcoholic with a raging temper. Della was sweet but had to face her demons, mental illness.

Yes, I will be the first one to say, they both had social problems that none one of their kids could understand. But they stayed together through thick and thin. That's what you call the love factor. Mr. Ed and Della's story highlights their love, as well as their tumultuous relationship. Some people might say, love hurts sometimes, I would say to them, but why do others have to suffer through their pain. Fighting, and loving, and making babies, that's all these two did, I can't understand the life of me, why they proceeded to have more kids that needed to be fed, it was just plain stupid.

Alcoholism is a major problem in itself. Then to have another parent suffering with mental illness. Their children wanted to pull all their hair out of their heads. It was just too much! The children endured the humiliation of one parent an alcoholic, and the other parent having mental problems. Who wants to explain why their father got drunk every Friday? It was crazy.

But Mr. Ed had his own way.

If I think back, Mr. Ed didn't converse much about his earlier years, but when he did, he talked about how mean his pops was. He said if he asked for extra food, his dad would say, "son, we ain't running no race,'' and that was that. He didn't get no extra food. But he had the same traits as his father. This he tried to avoid, because back in the day, Mr. Ed only ate the best, pork chops, which was a delicacy back in the day, while his children fought over a chicken breast. He didn't eat chicken. Josie remembered sneaking in the kitchen at night and getting a bite of Mr. Ed's pride and joy, his giant size pork chop and the bacon he flaunted in our faces. But this was payback, while he slept, I ate and ate until I couldn't eat another drop of food. How would he know anyway? Especially since he came home drunk and smelled like raw eggs, that was so foul, it made me want to throw up! All the things my father hated in is father, sadly he became a mean tyrant that got drunk and tormented his family, taking the life out of every bloom of flower we picked, leaving me with a spirit floating into a world of make believe.

Once in a while, Mr. Ed would say, "I don't want to be like my dad' because my father was a hateful person." Unfortunately, my father mirrored his father's traits, *like father, like son.*

Now back to Mr. Ed's mom, I don't have too much to say about grandma, but the little things I can say about her was she was a sweet low-key woman; she was light brown and very beautiful. But granddad, my dad's father they always talked about him being mean.

To keep the peace, grandma flattered her man with compliments appeasing his gigantic ego to avoid this ticking time bomb. It was her way of letting him shine not complaining about his imperfections while raising their kids. She loved her kids dearly. I remembered her gentleness; she was such a kind soul.

My father's parents were farmers; this is where my father met *The Love of His Life, Della.*

Growing up, Mr. Ed didn't have the luxury of getting a higher education. Therefore, he developed a skill and perfected it until he became the most skilled dancer in the area where he lived. He won so many trophies for his dancing, leaving no one to chance or to debate who was the best dancer around.

As I stated earlier, Della had two kids from her previous relationship, but Mr. Ed didn't care because he was smitten by her beauty. Della was medium built with bow legs that caused men to forget their thought or their purpose when she came around, Della was hot!

Mr. Ed got tongue tied when she was around him. He couldn't even speak. He just mumbled and made a fool out of himself.

At first, Della seemed annoyed by his presence but then she started noticing how handsome Mr. Ed was.

Then, one day, while they were picking cotton, Mr. Ed showed Della his moves, a song came on the radio, that he just couldn't shake, he jumped up, and fell on his knees and started rocking back on his legs like he was a rocking chair, everybody stopped and started cheering saying,

"Go Ed Go!" Then, Little Ed as he was called, grabbed Della and he rocked her back and forth and that my friend, *that's all she wrote*, Della was his from that point on. Della and Mr. Ed got married; Della had two boys from previous relationships, but to her dismay, none of her other relationships worked out well. Della was such a beautiful woman, she had a beautiful alluring smile, but poor Della, little did she know, Mr. Ed would test every emotion in her fragile body.

At first, Ed-Man behaved himself, after all, marriage was new to him, but then his true self came to light, and let me tell you, it wasn't pretty.

He started drinking corn liquor and whatever he could consume. You know what they say, alcohol brings your true self out and the demons in Mr. Ed was just about to be unleased and diverted on the ones he professed to love.

Mr. Ed was jealous of Della. Della couldn't look at another man. If she did, there were consequences behind her actions. A simple walk up the street caused a domino effect because this man didn't trust anyone. Even though he cheated on Della, he thought everyone was like him.

Even after Gigi came along, his first little girl, Mr. Ed couldn't control his anger. Nevertheless, he cherished Gigi and for a moment, he seemed to calm down. This was his first and my goodness, it was not going be the last child. Right after her, then came little Josie. He named her after his beautiful dark-skinned sister.

Later on in life, little Josie would be a thorn in her other sister's side and I speak that literally. Ed was slim built and one of the handsomest black men that could very much grace the cover of any magazine. Ed was super shy until he discovered his downfall, the big A, Alcohol. Alcohol gave him the courage to voice his thoughts with no shame of being misunderstood by anyone, and what alcohol couldn't do, his trigger finger silenced anyone that doubted Mr. Ed. He had the power.

If you had a beef with Mr. Ed your best bet was to act fast before you flutter your eyes, if not, a gun would be pointing in your face or a knife stuck in your back. It depended on what mood he was in at the time.

Mr. Ed loved music. And one of his favorite songs of all times were, *I Can't Get Next to You* by the Temptations.

Let me begin by introducing myself, my name is Josie the second daughter of Della and Mr. Ed.

Growing up in the early sixties, it was hard because my mother was diagnosed with a critical problem, mental illness. Seeing my mother experience this, I decided to coin a phrase, "The Big Bad Wolf. I used this phrase to highlight Della when she transformed into a fearless woman becoming "The Big Bad Wolf, it was during these bouts with mental illness, that

Della became a force that was so powerful that even Mr. Ed trembled to his knees!

I personally witnessed some of her transformations and thought this phrase most definitely represented Della's behavior during these explosive periods in our life.

When the creature came out, Della couldn't be contained because the beast couldn't be controlled. Well, let me tell you how this came about, one-night, the children had just witnessed Mr. Ed's, violent alcoholic rage and while he stormed through the door, soliciting anyone in his path to a fight; he was in another drunken stupor; he tumbled and fell with his head hitting the floor. I put my hands over my mouth to shield it from my laughter with a smug look on my face. Mr. Ed picked himself up and walked towards Della, and boy if his eyes could talk, it would have said, Run Della Run! Poor Della, she didn't deserve this, especially since she had worked hard in the fields that day and still managed to cook a delicious meal for her kids while awaiting Mr. Ed's return. But, little did she know, that from this **tumultuous** fight she would be deemed the Big Bad Wolf releasing a powerful robust creature that hid away tucked deep within her brain.

But let me get back to the story, Mr. Ed grabbed Della by the hair and started beating her non-stop with his fists, he cold cocked her several times in the face. Della tumbled to the floor while she yelled for her children to go in the other room and shut the door quick because Mr. Ed didn't care who he hit when he was drunk or in his private alcoholic rage. Poor Della, didn't want her children to see this again. Nevertheless, all of the kids scrambled to get in the adjoining rooms but Gigi was holding back this time. This little bitty girl was ready to jump, not fearing Mr. Ed. Gigi pushed us back because she was willing to step up and help Della beat this man up. The younger kids started crying while the next in line comforted their fears with a warm blanket.

All we could hear was yelling as this unpolitic man pounded on Della with a passion to do her harm. Josie closed her eyes and focused her thoughts on Della and praying that "The Big Bad Wolf would come out that night and devour this pitiful man. Mr. Ed, a man not fit to be called my father. Sadly, this was a ritual for this man. Most weekends when he came home, he felt the need to fight, and fight he did.

Mr. Ed worked in construction. He worked on bridges and highways in the county. Instead of being energized to bring joy to his family, he was motivated to do damage to his trusting family. Mr. Ed made a conscious effort to torture us all with his drinking cussing, fighting and fussing. But this night would be different for Mr. Ed, he was about to see the power behind this mild temper subservient woman. He was going to feel the fire and get what was due to him, this spineless man that was my father. Suddenly, we heard several strange sounds like someone was falling. We cracked the door anticipating the unexpected. It seemed eerily quiet, then suddenly, the door opened and Mr. Ed was fleeing from the living room, while his bottle of Jack Daniels fell to the floor and this man was terrified! What's going on? He looked very bewildered, but of what? All the kids looked back and that's when we saw my mother, Della. She had a weird look on her face, like an animal had replaced her face with a hardened criminal; it frightened me! Had the animal come out of Della? Yep, and I witnessed it firsthand. Della grabbed Mr. Ed and started tossing him in the air while this frighten creature struggled to free himself. He gave out a shriek, yelling, "please Della, stop, I am sorry!" His face looked like a tiger had been let loose on it, and boy I was beaming with excitement. It seemed this time, Mr. Ed was the one fighting for his life. A life that he made hell for all those at his mercy. Little did he know from that point on, "The Big Bad Wolf" would find a place for Della to reclaim the strength she needed to overpower this loser of her husband.

Oh, that night, it seemed that Della tortured Mr. Ed, throwing him every which way but up and she didn't care if she broke any bones. This was music to my ears. His drinking and bullying us around like we were his punching bags, and doing whatever he pleased was finally over. Finally, The Big Bad Wolf came out of Della, and all hell broke loose.

That night, I was ecstatic that my father, was getting the hell beat out of him. Della, grabbed him with her fist picking him up and threw his skinny butt outside. But before Della could come outside and finish giving him a good butt whooping, this skinny man had got the hell out of there, he started running and the only thing that was seen was his jacket flying in the wind.

A black stick in the darkness. I closed my eyes celebrating this victory, this was something all of us had been waiting for! This is what I've been praying about the longest time.

Ha Ha, Ha

And this was only the beginning, because what Mr. Ed didn't know Della was about to take back control of her life. This was not going to be the last of the beast coming out of Della. Although this was one victory for Della, there would be plenty more. Della had to go away to a mental facility for almost two months to heal her troubled mind.

{Grown Ed-Man, The Shot Houses and Mary Jo}

Mr. Ed earned a reputation at the shot houses. Once he walked in, it was just like in the movies, everyone eyeing him down. Men started holding their ladies tight, they truly were afraid they were about to lose them that night to Mr. Ed. He was that chocolate fella that women just loved to take a nip on. And boy they were right, because Mr. Ed didn't care who came in together. He was the man, and no one would get in his way of what he wanted, if they did, his knife was ready to slice up what his slick hands couldn't do. And size didn't matter the least, big, little, or super-size, he loved them all.

That night, at one of Mr. Ed favorite juke joints, the music was bumping and the atmosphere seemed inviting him to make his moves. Mr. Ed couldn't help himself while sliding across the floor, admiring himself while all the men started running in a state of panic trying to reclaim their missing women at the bar. Then there was a hushing sound that erupted as the charismatic Ed floated as if he had wings across the dance floor grabbing the first lady in his path. But before he could focus on anyone, Mary Jo bounced her big behind and snatched him up. This heavyweight lover wasn't about to let anyone get her man that night, oh nooooooooooooo! She was ready to slow roll until the midnight rolled in. Just in the nick of time, her favorite song came on, *I Will Never Love Another* by the Temptations. Never mind, Mr. Ed had a wife; this night was hers and hers alone. As the song played, Mr. Ed, grabbed Mary Jo squeezing her so tight she almost lost her breath while he whispered in her ear, "baby I will never love another like I'm loving you right now."

Poor Mary Jo almost fainted; she was powerless Mr. Ed had her strung out. The spell Mr. Ed had on her she couldn't shake loose. This time in space belonged only to Mr. Ed and that was all that mattered to Mary Jo. She dismissed the sore losers, she had her man, ah, doesn't it hurt? This man was hers tonight. May Jo didn't move even after receiving some of the most hateful looks. She just returned them a smug look, all but saying he is mines. Mary Jo was the envy of the ladies and she didn't have no regrets.

Then another song came on *Ain't No Way by Aretha Franklin*, Mary Jo, slow rolled her big behind around and around. Poor Mary Jo loved Mr. Ed. She knew Mr. Ed wasn't no good but she had to have him, this was the price she had to pay for loving a married man. Mr. Ed had something she couldn't turn loose. He knew how to make love to her, so tonight was her night and she was about to give him all that she had to give.

{Della's Breakdowns}

After Della released the Big Bad Wolf, she had to revisit the Mental Facility for rest, she took time to rest her mind. Actually, she got a good rest because she didn't have to jump when Mr. Ed said jump, even though she missed her kids, she needed this break.

Even though Della was isolated, she welcomed her space and time from Mr. Ed. He sucked the life out her, especially when he went on his drinking sprees. It was party time for him. Time to run, time to fight and argue.

This one particular day, Mr. Ed had arrived at the facility earlier than normal so that he could have more time with Della. Earlier when he was driving, he noticed a bad storm cloud but he dismissed the idea that he would be caught up in a rain storm.

After every visit with Della, he left feeling overwhelmed and the desperation was getting him down. Every time he left Della, she always screamed when he told her he had to leave. She would say, "don't let them keep me, please Ed." And every time, he begged Della to listen to the staff so she would be able to come home soon.

But the moment he started walking away, Della started running like a mad woman, kicking and fighting whoever was in her way to get out the door. This upset Ed but all he could do was bow his head.

One visit when Mr. Ed walked through the door dressed in a suit, a hat and red shoes, the women, old and young, turned around. One lady was bumping her head back and forth on her table, she stopped. A nurse was passing out medicine, she almost dropped her medication looking at that black cat with the red shoes, who was so smooth. He looked like a high class fellow that had a little money. Awe, she wetted her lips. Gotta taste this sweet chocolate delight.

The ladies started motioning him to come to their table, but Mr. Ed had one lady in mind, that was Della. Mr. Ed waited for the people to bring Della out.

On this visit, he and Della had just pulled up a table when his favorite song of all times started to play on the radio. Mr. Ed reminisced about the times he and Della danced until the morning. All of sudden, the spirit hit him and he started singing and dancing with the song, I **Will Never Love Another After Loving You by the Temptations**". The nurse at the station stopped the music and Mr. Ed sung his heart out to his lady love Della. Even Della started singing, and she hit a note or two with him. Mr. Ed started to dance, he showed his fancy foot work and the whole building gave him a standing ovation.

Even the woman that was bumping her head, stopped and threw him a kiss. But Mr. Ed's attention was only on Della. When he finished dancing, Mr. Ed gave Della another passionate kiss. This time he shoved his tongue down her throat. Oh, no, Della didn't mind, this was her man! And she had to give him what he wanted. But before she had time to give him a second kiss, she had to go to the bathroom. When she walked to the bathroom, the other patients, and nurses surrounded Mr. Ed. They just couldn't help themselves; he did a split and jumped on his knees and rocked and rocked back and forth sending the people into to a frenzy. Several nurses and patients gave him their number, oh yes, he loved Della, but he loved doing the do equally as much. Mr. Ed was addicted to sex. The more he got, the more he wanted.

You would think these women were used to men, but this midnight joy was handsome and his moves spelled out excitement. These ladies continued to throw kisses even when Della walked back, just in time to catch someone eying her man. Oh No! She walked up to one of the patients and slapped her so hard, the woman turned around and around.

The poor lady ran screaming. The guards came not before Della grabbed her man, and tongued him down, "This Is My Man she yelled out, "nobody better look at him!" Della balled up one of her fists.

The guards grabbed Della, and Della started fighting and knocking everyone out. Mr. Ed couldn't watch this. He begged Della to be quiet. "Time to go," the attendant told Mr. Ed, then like before all hell broke loose.

Della started screaming and fighting the attendants, saying, "Please Ed, don't go!" All Mr. Ed could do was **Walk Away from Love** a song made famous by the Temptations.

Oh! the tears he had fought back came pouring down, he loved this woman; even though he treated her badly when she was home, he loved her dearly. They shared good memories as well. Mr. Ed looked back and saw the attendants grab his wife and escort her back to her room. How could he ever love someone like he loved Della? He loved her despite his abusive actions. Ed loved Della despite her illness. There was no one on this earth that he loved more than Della. Even though this included all the affairs, and there certainly were many and still counting. But there had not been another woman in his life that could compare to the love he had for Della.

Della screamed out, "Ed, don't leave me?" Then, an involuntary reflex from his brain kicked in, and Mr. Ed started running, and the more he ran, this song kept ringing deep in his soul, *"the song got louder and louder. "I Could Never Love Another After Loving You by the Temptations."*

Ed, ran and ran, he didn't mind the rain that was beating down on his skinny body, soaking his clothes and cleaning that musk from his shirt. All he knew was that he had to get away He was powerless against the Big Bad Wolf that Della kept locked up in her brain.

Every time the wolf came out, Della had to be transported back to this place to get some treatment. Della's strength surpassed ten men when she was going through her bouts with mental illness. Mr. Ed could attest to that because Della beat the mess out of him when the Big Bad Wolf took over her body. Even Della's fist was powerful and she hammed it on Mr. Ed, her husband.

Well, let's see how the Big Bad Wolf, slowly took over Della's thoughts. It didn't happen by chance. There were a number of factors. The main factor was Mr. Ed's drinking and abusive behavior. Every time Mr. Ed said he was going to treat Della better, he regressed back into his old pattern, drinking, raising hell and fighting. My gosh, Mr. Ed loved Della but the bottle had him under a spell and it strung him along like a puppet.

Well, let me get back to how Della ended up in the Big Bad Wolf's claws. Mr. Ed's job required him to work away from home during the week. He came home on weekends. When he came home, he always had to celebrate by going out with the boys, usually it involved drinking. I guess a little fun is due, but for Mr. Ed, he came home ready to ruff someone up and it was usually his wife Della.

You know it wouldn't be Mr. Ed if he didn't drink all night and come home the next morning, but one time he came home early and when he raised his fist to slap Della, she grabbed him and started beating the shit out of him. Where did this strength come from, then Mr. Ed realized, the Big Bad Wolf had come out again. She wasn't acting like she normally acted, Della calmed down and told Mr. Ed to follow her outside. He proceeded to go.

There, Della gazed up at the sky while she talked in a language only a fool could understand. She transfixed her eyes upward just staring. Mr. Ed was frozen with fear because Della's strength surpassed his when the Big Bad Wolf controlled her body. He was actually afraid to move fearing Della would knock him out cold. Della became a prize fighter when the Big Bad Wolf was released. So again, she had to go back to get some rest.

This was the last time Della would let the Big Bad Wolf come out. Della was medicated to relieve her stress and her faith helped her deal with Mr. Ed's rage and his temper.

Gigi had gotten older, and she'd be damned that she'd see Mr. Ed hit Della for no reason at all. She was willing to bite the bullet because Mr. Ed's destructive behavior had gone on too long. Gigi had been the target of his rage, because she almost got sliced up by an ax Mr. Ed had thrown, missing her small body by only an inch. But Gigi had no fear, Mr. Ed had toughened her up to withstand anything. She had looked fear in the eyes and stood not batting an eye. What about Josie? Well, any signs of trouble, Josie hid. Josie watched her father Mr. Ed practice what he was going to say before he reached the house. Saying out loud, I'm going to make Della pay. But for what, he was the one who acted like a fool all the time. And let us not forget about Dana, she sucked up to all the older women in the neighborhood; Dana would go and visit all the older ladies in the neighborhood and when she came home, she had lots of treats. Dana was so good at what she did, she would brag about what she said to these older ladies. She got clothes, food and money. The rest of the children hung around her as she distributed her treats.

When we got older, every summer we had to work the fields to get our school clothes, but Mr. Ed only bought about two dresses, a pair of shoes and one slip and one pack of underwear for the whole school year. We had to wash our clothes every night. Since we were the same size, we switched up our clothing. Mother made sure we all were cleaned despite not having a lot of clothes.

Our Teen Years

When we became teenagers, the fun started. We were so naïve about the pleasures of life. Dana started dating first, then Gigi and finally,

Josie. Our house was the hot spot; we would get some popcorn, cool aid, and invite our friends over and the party was on. Times were so different back then, friends came over and just had good clean fun, nothing crazy. All we wanted to do was dance, we danced and danced. We had a house filled with kids, no smoking or drinking were ever involved. We just wanted to dance and mingle.

One boy at school asked what's going on at your house, Josie. I laughed and said, nothing but dancing. Of course, he didn't believe it, but that's all that was going on.

The girls would try to out dance the boys but the boys would come back strong. One night, Mr. Ed had come home and the noise had gotten to him, would you believe that man pulled out his pistol and shot into the ceiling? The boys scattered everywhere, leaving us in disbelief. Two big rats fell down out of the ceiling that ended the party that night. All our guests were jumping around trying to avoid the gigantic rats. This was so embarrassing that we had to stop having people over for a while.

Mr. Ed liked taking us to some of his favorite hot spots, liquor houses. That was the only place he seemed to be at home, because he enjoyed flirting and disrespecting other men's women.

But if anyone looked sideways at Della, Mr. Ed wanted to fight. How hypocritical? One night, Mr. Ed got stuck in the woods with big fat Mary. Like I said, he liked all sizes of women. Mr. Ed and his lady friend had to hitch a ride back home. But he didn't care, he had done what he wanted to do.

I recalled one time, Mr. Ed and his buddy was sharing a woman when a heated argument broke out between the two, they started fighting about who woman she was. How bout this fool was a married man. This man had no shame in his game. You would think Mr. Ed would have changed, but his behavior continued when he got older. It is rumored that he fathered another child, not sure if this is true or not.

Mr. Ed, had an accident one day, and the police came out to inspect his vehicle. They asked him did he have any license, Mr. Ed smiled and said, "I drank them up.

The officers just burst out laughing.

All the children had grown up, and now Mr. Ed had grandchildren and guess what, he took every last one of them to his favorite spot. He would get so drunk; that the teenager had to drive him home. Mr. Ed knew the kids had no license.

Sometimes, the grandchildren had to defend Mr. Ed because as you know, he was always trying to get some man's lady. He didn't care if

the woman came in with the man. Oh, no!
Everyone was free game for Mr. Ed.

But as the years came and went, Mr. Ed's
health declined. His mind was still strong in that
he remembered everything, but the years of
abusing alcohol had damaged his liver.
Meanwhile, Della's health had declined also; she
was having problems with her knees.

All the children had moved out, but the
children came over regularly to help Della and
Mr. Ed out.

Della had two knee replacements, but instead
of exercising, she decided not to and this caused
her knees to lock up and she lost the ability to
walk. Mr. Ed's health was getting worse, he was
no longer able to take a good bath and had to rely
on his daughter Josie to help assist him with his
other personal needs.

One day, Josie for some reason, had a weird
feeling, it wasn't her time to go over her parent's
house to help with their baths but she decided to
go that day. When she arrived, her mother said,
"Josie please go and check on your father
because he told me, he was going in his room to
die." Josie ran to check out her father. There on
the floor, she found him lying face down. He
struggled to get to his room because he didn't
want his woman to see him die.

Mr. Ed had finally found peace.

My life changed after that because losing a parent is devastating. I loved my father dearly despite his addiction.

Sometimes we don't miss a person until they are dead and gone. He had lived a life without any regrets. But he never conquered his problem with the bottle.

Mr. Ed, my father was loved especially by his grandchildren. After all, they got a history lesson. Mr. Ed educated them on women, booze and how to work and take care of a family. He added to their lives and spread his wisdom by telling his children stories.

Sadly, Mr. Ed lived his life on his on terms, but his imagination, he gifted it to his daughter, Josie. He also, never forgot what his forefathers had taught him and passed his knowledge down to his children, strong work ethics. If he had only realized that corn liquor was a tool the white man used against the blacks to humiliate them. If he only knew that he had a heritage that produced strong black people and that gift was in his blood

The question posed to you, did Mr. Ed tell me the story. Let me say this. He told us tales about when Herbert Hoover was president and how the government had to give out food. He said, "Herbert Hoover was the worse president ever.

His wisdom was priceless.

He loved us all.

THE BRONZE PLANTATION AND MR. ED
My mom had to overcome so many hurdles suffering with a disease that caused her so much pain. But she used that and dished out so much love, she was the best mom ever!

She instilled in me the meaning of love; she had a heart that would melt the soul.

Chapter Five: Relevant Information about History

My intake on the Uncle Toms
In the story I mentioned Uncle Toms. Why these slaves ran and told their masters everything, I think because they were conditioned. Some probably thought they were doing the right thing while others were self-seeking for their own needs. Then there were others who probably pretended to be Uncle Toms for the greater good. Maybe he portrayed to be submissive only to gain the master's trust. But he knew he had to tell on someone, it may be for his own survival. I'm sure there were causalities along the way. He sought to gain the master's trust in order for the master to reveal his plans.

But today, there are modern day Uncle Toms;

I remembered an election was coming up and someone knocked on my door, I looked out and there were two black ladies petitioning support for this white mayor. I told them, "We have not had a black mayor since I can remember. They stop and then said, "the person was paying them great," that's why they were out soliciting for his support. I shook my head.

Black people are still willing to be bought.

We see it today, with so-called black conservatives, some are willing to sacrifice, other blacks to gain approval by the white man. **Educate yourself, look up these words!** Conductor

- Contrabands
- Emancipation
- Operative
- Slave patrol
- Middle passage
- 3th Amendment, this abolished slavery Dec. 6, 1865
- Abolitionist-anti-slavery activist
- African Diaspora-the dispersal of Africans in the new world
- Bleeding Kansas
- Bondsperson
- Coffle-group of slaves transported for sale
- Chattel
- Peace Democrat
- Personal Liberty Law
- Redemption
- Fugitives
- Station
- Station masters
- Manumit-freeing enslaved by will

•   recession
We must never forget
Educate yourself by researching these
Massacres!
   Tulsa Race Riot 199
   Wilmington Insurrection of 1898
   New York City Draft Riots
   Red Summer Riot 1919
   Opelousas Massacre 1868
   New Orleans Massacre of 1866
   Atlanta Race Riots
   Rosewood Massacre
   Ocoee Massacre, known as Sundown Town

Songs that inspired us

The Impossible Dream by Joe Darion Mitchell Leigh

To dream the impossible dream
To fight the unbeatable foe
To bear with unbearable sorrow
To run where the brave dare not go
To right the unrightable wrong
To love pure and chaste from afar
To try when your arms are too weary
To reach the unreachable star
This is my quest, to follow that star,

No matter how hopeless, no matter how far
to fight for the right without question or cause
To be willing to march into hell for a heavenly
cause. And I know if I'll only be true to this
glorious quest
That my heart will lie peaceful and calm when
I'm laid to my rest and the world will be better
for this That one man scorned and covered with
scars Still strove with his last ounce of courage
To fight the unbeatable foe, to reach the
unreachable star

Change Gonna Come penned
by Sam Cooke

I was born by the <u>river</u> in a <u>little</u> tent
Oh, and just like the <u>river</u> I've been <u>running</u> ev'r
since
It's been a long time, a long time coming
But I know a <u>change</u> gonna come, oh yes it will
It's been too hard living, but I'm <u>afraid</u> to die
Cause I don't know what's up there, <u>beyond</u> the
sky<u>.</u> It's been a long, a long time coming
But I know a <u>change</u> gonna come, oh yes it will
I go to the <u>movie</u> and I go downtown
Somebody keeps telling' me don't hang around
It's been a long, a long time coming
But I know a <u>change</u> gonna come, oh yes it will
Then I go to my brother
And I say <u>brother</u> help me please

But he <u>winds</u> up knocking' me
Back down on my knees, oh
There have been <u>times</u> that I <u>thought</u> I couldn't
last for long But now I <u>think</u> I'm able to <u>carry</u> on
It's been a long, a long time coming
But I know a <u>change</u> is <u>gonna</u> come, oh yes it
will
https://www.songfacts.com/facts/marvin-gaye/whats-going-on
What is going on was written by three buddies, that were hitmakers; songwriter Al Cleveland, Four Tops member Renaldo "Obie Benson and Singer Marvin Gaye who added lyrics and worked on the arrangement. Gaye wanted the Originals to record the song, but Benson and Cleveland prevailed upon Gaye to do it himself

**What Going on by
Al Cleveland, Renaldo of Four
Tops and Marvin Gaye**

Mother, mother
There's too many of you crying
Brother, brother, brother
There's far too many of you dying
You know we've got to find a way
To bring some Lovin' here today, eh eh
Father, father

We don't need to escalate
You see, war is not the answer
For only love can conquer hate
You know we've got to find a way
To bring some lovin' here today, oh oh oh
Picket lines and picket signs
Don't punish me with brutality
C'mon talk to me
So you can see
What's going on
Yeah, what's going on
Tell me what's going on
I'll tell you what's going on, ooh ooh ooh ooh
Right on baby
Right on baby

1.   Swing Low, Sweet Chariot

Swing Low, Sweet Chariot is a renowned call
and response black gospel song in which the
preacher sings the first line and the congregation
responds. When a slave heard this tune, he would
know that he had to be prepared for the big
escape. The song talks about an angel band that
takes the slave to freedom. The Sweet Chariot is
a code name for The Underground Railroad
which comes south (*swing low*) to take the slave
to the free north (*carry me home*).

2.   Wade in the Water

Wade in the Water is a Negro spiritual song that teaches slaves to hide and make it through by getting into the water. It's a perfect map song example with lyrics that offer precious coded directions.

3.   Steal Away

This song's message is that the one singing it is planning to break free from enslavement. The lyrics say the Lord calls the slave to freedom and that there's not much time left to stay on the plantation.

4.   Amazing Grace

This famous melody was written by a captain of a slave ship. *Amazing Grace* is often attributed to another old slave tune and was originally played on the piano black keys in order to give it a sorrowful vibe. Now, this black gospel song is a staple at churches and funerals.

5.   Follow the Drinkin' Gourd

The drinking gourd mentioned in this African American gospel folk song is actually a water dipper which is the Big Dipper's code name. The Big Dipper points towards the north, to the Pole Star. As moss only grows on the dead trees' north side, the Big Dipper will guide the slaves north. *Follow the Drinkin' Gourd* also suggests escaping during spring since days get longer and the quails start calling each other in April.

6.   Go Down Moses

Go Down Moses talks about the Bible's Old Testament events, particularly Exodus 8:1. In the lyrics, Israel means African American slaves
while Pharaoh and Egypt mean the slave master. The word *down*, in the American slavery context, means *down the Mississippi river*, the place where slaves had to struggle with awful conditions. It is easy to see the roots of this black gospel song.

7.   **Nobody Knows the Trouble I've Seen**
This masterpiece originated during the slavery period but was published in 1867, in a book entitled *Slave Songs of the United States*. Many artists such as Louis Armstrong, Marian Anderson, and Sam Cooke have done cover versions of the song. This is one of the most popular black gospel songs.

8.   **Thorny Desert**
A version of this gospel hymn was sung **by Harriet Tubman**, an abolitionist and political activist, to signal her presence to the slaves who were looking for her help to escape.

9.   **Let Us Break Bread Together**
The roots of this song were probably formed in the slave culture that developed in South-Eastern colonial America's coastal areas such as South Carolina, St. Helena Island, Charleston, and Beaufort. *Let Us Break Bread Together* is a call

for Christians to come together, whether knelt or stood and celebrate the Lord's Supper.

10.   Song of the Free

Written in 1860, *Song of the Free* was composed to the *Oh! Susanna* tune. It talks about a slave man who fled slavery in Tennessee. The protagonist managed to escape to Canada by using the Underground Railroad.

11.   Down in the River to Pray

While its exact origin remains unknown, research suggests that *Down in the River to Pray* was written by a slave. The phrase *in the river* (sometimes replaced by *to the river*) represents a coded slavery escaping message. When slaves fled, they'd walk in the river to cover their scent from the bounty-hunters' dogs.

In addition, *starry crown* can mean navigating the slaves' escape by the stars and *Good Lord, show me the way* might be a prayer for finding the Underground Railroad.

12.   Michael Row the Boat Ashore

Former slaves whose masters had left the island prior to the Union navy arrival that enforced a blockage sang *Michael Row the Boat Ashore*. Charles Pickard Ware, a Harvard graduate and abolitionist, was supervising St. Helena Island's plantations between 1862 and 1865.

During that time, he noted this song down right as he heard it sang by the freedmen. In 1863, his cousin, William Francis Allen, reported that the former slaves were singing this song while they rowed him in a boat over Station Creek. That's why this is one of the most historical black gospel songs.

13.   Sometimes I Feel Like a Motherless Child

This traditional Negro spiritual dates back to the slavery era. *Sometimes I Feel Like a Motherless Child* expresses despair and pain. Furthermore, it conveys the lack of hope of a child who's been torn from the parents.

The word *sometimes* is repeated several times, which can be interpreted as a measure of hope, as it suggests that occasionally this child doesn't feel motherless. This child can represent a slave who, in the trafficking process, has been separated from something dear to his or her heart (such as a spouse, home country, parents, children, siblings, and so on) and is yearning for it.

14.   Didn't My Lord Deliver Daniel

Didn't My Lord Deliver Daniel is a song that expresses an enslaved man's conflicting thoughts. Unlike most gospel songs, these lyrics manifest disappointment, irony, and humor in reaction to the absurd nature of life as it was experienced by slaves. On the other hand, it may be just someone looking at the suffering going on around them and wondering why doesn't God save everyone on Earth since he made the effort to save Daniel.

15.   The Gospel Train

While the language used in *The Gospel Train* apparently describes regular activities, its second meaning can easily be related to the Underground Railroad.

16.   Mary, Don't You Weep

Originating from earlier than the American Civil War, *Mary Don't You Weep* is one of the essential Negro spirituals, as it contains coded opposition and hope messages. It is exactly what scholars call a label describing their roots among the enslaved as well as an authentic slave song.

17.   He Never Said a Mumblin'Word

He Never Said a Mumblin 'Word is a spiritual folk gospel song also known as Easter, They Hung Him on a Cross, Crucifixion, and Mumblin' Word. It narrates Jesus Christ's crucifixion, giving a detailed description of the event. The origins of this work are unknown; however, many think that it dates back to the slavery period.

18.   Roll, Jordan, Roll

Roll, Jordan, Roll is, undoubtedly, a staple in gospel music. The song was written by Charles Wesley and became famous among the slaves during the 19th century, being created as an escape coded message.

19.   We Are Climbing Jacob's Ladder

One of the first slave spirituals that became popular among white Christians, *We Are Climbing Jacob's Ladder* is a masterpiece that, according to academics, was written somewhere between 1750 and 1825. The song is based on Jacob's ladder Biblical story and its lyrics hold out hope that the enslaved can escape and enjoy freedom. Numerous artists have recorded remarkable versions of it and it was even used as one of the principal themes in the great documentary entitled *The Civil War*.

20.   Free at Last

This simple Negro spiritual has a straightforward point, as shown in the following lyrics: *Free at last, free at last/I thank God I'm free at last*. Moreover, its significance was proven by Rev. Martin Luther King, Jr.'s quotation in his world-famous *I Have a Dream* speech from 1963. It has one of the most memorable lines from all the black gospel songs.

21.   I Got a Robe

Envisioning the freedom in Heaven, *I Got a Robe* is another key gospel song that many say is rooted in the slavery era.

22.   He's Just the Same Today

He's Just the Same Today mainly talks about God's constancy. Nevertheless, the choice of examples (Daniel's refusal to *bow down to men* as well as the Hebrews' escape from bondage) gives a subtext of pro-freedom.

23.   Jesus On the Waterside

Many believe that *Jesus on The Waterside* is a slave song. Its lyrics can either mean becoming

free by dying and going to heaven or simply by escaping slavery via the Underground Railroad. In both situations, *Jesus will be sittin' on de water-side*, helping the enslaved succeed.

24.   There is a Balm in Gilead

This is a traditional Negro spiritual sang by members of the contraband camp as Charlotte Jenkins was arriving for the very first time to the Mansion House Hospital. By singing at contrabands camps, former slaves managed to navigate the area between enslavement and freedom.

25.   I'm on My Way to Canaan Land

Just like other Negro spirituals, *I'm on My Way to Canaan Land* has a dual meaning for slaves. The word *Canaan* doesn't only mean Heaven, but also north, and particularly the British colonies that later became Canada. That was the place where fugitive slaves were going in order to be free. These are just some of the truly inspiring black gospel songs written and sung by slaves in America facing unimaginable pain.

Sexual abuse of black women during slavery in America. "SLAVERY is terrible for men; but it is far more terrible for women," Harriet Jacobs in Systemic Racism.

During slavery, the black African woman was regarded as an object of economic value.

At the same time, she was also treated as an object of sexual abuse by white slave owners. There was a belief that a black woman was sexually promiscuous and she could be raped and abused at the slave master's will. Although information on the everyday life of a slave woman is scarce, there are a number of narratives and fictional writings that give us an insight into the past lives of women during slavery. Harriet Jacobs wrote the Systemic Racism. Jacobs was the first black woman to write a slave narrative in 1861.

Initially, the book was ascribed to Lydia Maria Child a white abolitionist. It was only 30 years ago when research showed that the book was written by a woman slave. This book provides insight and depth into the sexual exploitation of black women during slavery.

Harriet Jacobs noted the brutalization of black girls and women by white slave-masters, who justified their cruelty by viewing black women

as sexual savages.
The women were continuously stripped, beaten, raped and forced to 'breed' more children to keep the slave system going. As a result, black women suffered a double burden of slavery because of this sexual vulnerability.
In the fictionalized novel based on a character called Linda Brent, the main character explains that her slave master was a physician named Dr Flint who subjected her to sexual and physical abuse.
Jacobs also goes into detail about the violence of North Carolina slave owners.
She quotes a woman slave who said, "Pity me, and pardon me, O virtuous reader!
"You never knew what it is like to be a slave; to be entirely unprotected by law or custom; to have the laws reduce you to the condition of a chattel, entirely subject to the will of another.
"You never exhausted your ingenuity in avoiding the snares, and eluding the power of a hated tyrant; you never shuddered at the sound of his footsteps, and trembled within hearing of his
  voice. "Colonial laws regulating rape were not applied to black people or Indians.
This meant that Indians and blacks could not defend themselves against forms of abuse by white males. If a black woman accused her master of rape, she was subjected to more

beatings by the master or the madam.
There are many other stories of known political figures who took advantage of black women and fathered children. The late senator and segregationist Strom Thurmond, at the age of 22, had a child with a 16-year-old black girl who worked for his parents.
Thomas Jefferson also had a child with his slave, Sally Hemings. A recent genealogy study revealed that Michelle Obama was the great, great, great, granddaughter of a slave from Georgia called Melvinia.
At the age of age 15, Melvinia had a child with a white father who was most likely to have been the slave owner's son. In Quentin Tarantino's film 'Django Unchained, 'the producer focused mainly on the downtrodden lives of enslaved women named Eliza, Patsey, and Harriet. All three women are sexually subjected to rape by white men. In the film, Eliza played by Adepero Oduye was kept as the enslaved mistress of her slave owner master for nine years. At one stage, she confessed: "I have done dishonorable things to survive. "God forgive me."Eliza submitted to this treatment in order to secure a better life for her and the children. When the slave owner died, Eliza and her two children were sold to slave traders by the slave owner's daughter. A review of the film

notes that Eliza's young child Emily was sold as a 'fancy girl' because mulatto or light-skinned girls were sold purely for sexual labor and popular in the New Orleans slave market.
The slave trader remarks that there are, "heaps and piles of money to be made from her, she's a beauty. "Emily is both the product of white male sexual assault, and its future victim."
Harriet played by Alfre Woodard is also kept as a mistress, of Master Shaw, a nearby slave plantation owner.
At one stage Harriet confides that she accepts the master's 'pantomime' of affection because it keeps her safe. In another recent film called 12 Years A Slave', we find a slave girl called Patsey played by Lupita Nyong'o who is the key actress in the film being sexually abused by the master and physically beaten by the mistress.
But the question to ask is: why did the white women also abuse black women?
Some of the answers are found in recent history books. The historian, Gloria Browne-Marshall wrote a book titled, Failing Our Black Children: Statutory Rape Laws, Moral Reform and the Hypocrisy of Denial.
In book she noted that the white women were:
"Powerless against a lustful husband and blind to the harsh realities of chattel slavery, the enraged wife often vented her jealous rage upon the one

person whom she could control, the black woman." The everyday life experience of enslaved women was a painful survival of extreme labor, family destruction, sexual abuse and violence. Although little has been written about these abuses of black women during slavery, the fact remains that the plantation slave masters raped women.

These slave narratives of everyday life, form a most significant part of reclaiming the truth about the lives of black women during slavery.

**Must Read!
Emancipation: Promise and Poverty**

For African Americans in the South, life after slavery was a world transformed. Gone were the brutalities and indignities of slave life, the whippings and sexual assaults, the selling and forcible relocation of family members, the denial of education, wages, legal marriage, homeownership, and more. African Americans celebrated their newfound freedom both privately and in public jubilees.

But life in the years after slavery also proved to be difficult. Although slavery was over, the brutalities of white race prejudice persisted. After slavery, state governments across the South instituted laws known as **Black Codes**.

These laws granted certain legal rights to blacks, including the right to marry, own property, and sue in court, but the Codes also made it illegal for blacks to serve on juries, testify against whites, or serve in state militias. The Black Codes also required black sharecroppers and tenant farmers to sign annual labor contracts with white landowners. If they refused, they could be arrested and hired out for work.

Most southern black Americans, though free, lived in desperate rural poverty. Having been denied education and wages under slavery, ex-slaves were often forced by the necessity of their economic circumstances to rent land from former white slave owners. These **sharecroppers** paid rent on the land by giving a portion of their crop to the landowner.

In a few places in the South, former slaves

Family, Faith, and Education

Family, church, and school became centers of black life after slavery. With slavery's end, black women often preferred to be homemakers, though poverty pushed many blacks into the workforce. Black churches became centerpieces of African American culture and community, not only as places of personal spiritual renewal and communal worship but also as centers for learning, socializing, and political organization. Black ministers were community leaders.

African Americans' desire for education found expression in the establishment of schools at every level, from grade schools for basic-education to the founding of the nation's first black colleges such as Fisk University and Howard University. The **Freedmen's Bureau** (1865-1870), a government agency established to aid former slaves, oversaw some 3,000 schools across the South, and ran hospitals and healthcare facilities for the freedmen.

Reconstruction

During the period of **Reconstruction**, which lasted from 1865 to 1877, Congress passed and enforced laws that promoted civil and political rights for African Americans across the South. Most notable among the laws Congress passed were three Amendments to the US Constitution: The **Thirteenth Amendment** (1865) ended slavery, the **Fourteenth Amendment** (1868) guaranteed African Americans the rights of American citizenship, and the **Fifteenth Amendment** (1870) guaranteed black men the constitutional right to vote. African Americans actively took up the rights, opportunities, and responsibilities of citizenship. During Reconstruction, seven hundred African

American men served in elected public office, among them two United States Senators, and fourteen members of the United States House of Representatives. Another thirteen hundred African American men and women held appointed government jobs. **The KKK and the end of Reconstruction** From the late 1860s white supremacists in the **KKK** (Ku Klux Klan) terrorized African American leaders and citizens in the South until, in 1871, the US Congress passed legislation that resulted in the arrest and imprisonment of Klan leaders and the end of the Klan's terrorism of Americans for a time.

But over the course of the late 1860s and throughout the 1870s, the federal government's military presence was withdrawn from various southern states, and with the <u>Compromise of 1877</u>, **President Rutherford B. Hayes ordered the last federal troops in the South to** withdraw. With no troops to enforce the Fourteenth and Fifteen Amendments, Reconstruction was at an end. Across the South lynching, disenfranchisement, and segregationist laws proliferated. It would not be until after the Second World War and the 1960s **<u>Civil Rights Movement</u> that <u>Jim Crow segregation</u> would be** outlawed. Was 400 years ago, "about the latter end of August," that an English privateer ship reached Point Comfort on the

Virginia peninsula. There, Governor George Yeardley and his head of trade, Cape Merchant Abraham Piersey, bought the "20. and odd Negroes" aboard in exchange for "victuals" — meaning, they traded food for slaves. Such a trade, as described five months after the fact in a letter to the Virginia Company of London, had never before occurred in English North America, making this an ignominious milestone — and one that 400 years later is still surrounded by misconceptions and debate.

At the very least, 1619 represented a landmark in the long history of slavery in European colonies, and the beginning stages of what would become the institution of slavery in America. The New York *Times* this past weekend announced a special project **devoted to its indelible mark on American** society, and Hampton, Va., is commemorating the anniversary through Wednesday. Previously, on July 30, when President Trump spoke in Williamsburg, Va., to mark the 400th anniversary of Virginia's General Assembly, he noted — in a speech boycotted by the Virginia Legislative Black Caucus, over Trump's comments about black politicians — that it wasn't long after that governing body first met that the colony saw "the beginning of a barbaric trade in human lives."

How can we do a book about and leave information out about the Uncle Toms, this is how this character originated.

The term Uncle Tom, for those of you who don't know, actually originates with a character from a novel that was later made into a movie. Harriet Beecher Stowe published her novel Uncle Tom's Cabin in 1852. As an avid abolitionist, Stowe penned the novel as an anti-slavery message, highlighting the horror, cruelty, and inhumanity of slavery in the hopes of making the reasons slavery should be abolished tangible to millions. Her mission succeeded, and it is even said to have been one of the major catalytic forces behind the Civil War. In her novel, Uncle Tom was a placid, ever humble and ever subservient slave, who also happened to be quite competent. The focus that was later taken from the Uncle Tom character was his blindly faithful and ever loyal behavior when it came to his Master. So, you can imagine exactly what the black community felt about this character. A general summary can be found in the dictionary definition of what Uncle Tom means today:

What is an uncle Tom?

a black person who is eager to win the approval of white people and willing to cooperate with them

a black who is overeager to win the approval of whites (as by obsequious behavior or uncritical acceptance of white values and goals)

a member of a low-status group who is overly subservient to or cooperative with authority

BY <u>KEHINDE ANDREWS</u>15th March 2019

The slave master took Tom and dressed him well, and fed him well, and even gave him a little education; gave him a long coat and a top hat and made all the other slaves look up to him. Then he used tom to control them. The same strategy that wa used in those days is used today. He takes a Negro, so-called Negro, and makes him prominent, builds him up, publicizes him, makes him a celebrity. And then he becomes a spokesman for Negroes'

BY <u>JESSE GREENSPAN</u>

1. Isaac Hopper

Abolitionist Isaac Hopper

Kean Collection/Getty Images

Quakers played a huge role in the formation of the Underground Railroad, with George Washington complaining as early as 1786 that a "society of Quakers, formed for such purposes, have attempted to liberate" a neighbor's slave. Anti-slavery sentiment was particularly prominent in Philadelphia, where Isaac Hopper, a convert to Quakerism, established what one author called "the first operating cell of the abolitionist underground." In addition to hiding runaways in his own home, Hopper organized a network of safe havens and cultivated a web of informants so as to learn the plans of fugitive slave hunters. Though a tailor by trade, he also excelled at exploiting legal loopholes to win enslaved people's freedom in court. A friend of Joseph Bonaparte, the exiled brother of the former French emperor, Hopper moved to New York City in 1829. There, he continued helping escaped slaves, at one point fending off an anti-abolitionist mob that had gathered outside his Quaker bookstore.

2. John Brown

Abolitionist John Brown, c. 1846

Like his father before him, John Brown actively partook in the Underground Railroad, harboring runaways at his home and warehouse and establishing an anti-slave catcher militia following the 1850 passage of the Fugitive Slave Act. With several of his sons, he then participated in the so-called "Bleeding Kansas" conflict, leading one 1856 raid that resulted in the murder of five pro-slavery settlers. Another raid in December 1858 freed 11 enslaved people from three Missouri plantations, after which Brown took his hotly pursued charges on a nearly 1,500-mile journey to Canada. Becoming ever more radicalized, Brown's final action took place in October 1859, when he and 21 followers seized the federal armory in Harpers Ferry, Virginia (now West Virginia), in an attempt to foment a large-scale slave rebellion. Caught and quickly convicted, Brown was hanged to death that December.

3. Harriet Tubman
Born enslaved on Maryland's Eastern Shore, Harriet Tubman **endured constant brutal beatings, one of** which involved a two-pound lead weight and left her suffering from seizures and headaches for the rest of her life.

Worried that she would be sold and separated from her family, Tubman fled bondage in 1849, following the North Star on a 100-mile trek into Pennsylvania. Nicknamed "Moses," she went on to become the Underground Railroad's most famous "conductor," embarking on about 13 rescue operations back into Maryland and pulling out at least 70 enslaved people, including several siblings. A master of ingenious tricks, such as leaving on Saturdays, two days before slave owners could post runaway notices in the newspapers, she boasted of having never lost a single passenger. Tubman continued her anti-slavery activities during the Civil War, serving as a scout, spy and nurse for the Union Army

and even reportedly becoming the first U.S. woman to lead troops into battle.

4. Thomas Garrett

Thomas Garrett

The New York Public Library

On the way north, Tubman often stopped at the Wilmington, Delaware, home of her friend Thomas Garrett, a Quaker "stationmaster" who claimed to have aided some 2,750 fugitive slaves prior to the outbreak of the Civil War. Along with a place to stay, Garrett provided his visitors with money, clothing and food and sometimes personally escorted them arm-in-arm to a safer location. Occupational hazards included threats from pro-slavery advocates and a hefty fine imposed on him in 1848 for violating fugitive slave laws. Yet he determinedly carried on. "I should have done violence to my convictions of duty, had I not made use of all the lawful means in my power to liberate those people," he said in court, adding that "if any of you know of any poor slave who needs assistance, send him to me,

as I now publicly pledge myself to double my diligence and never neglect an opportunity to assist a slave to obtain freedom."

5. William Still

Hulton Archive/Getty Images

From Wilmington, the last Underground Railroad station in the slave state of Delaware,

many runaways made their way to the office of William Still in nearby Philadelphia. A free-born African American, Still chaired the Vigilance Committee of the Pennsylvania Abolition Society, which gave out food and clothing, coordinated escapes, raised funds and otherwise served as a one-stop social services shop for hundreds of fugitive slaves each year. Recording the personal histories of his visitors, Still eventually published a book that provided great insight into how the Underground Railroad operated. One arrival to his office turned out to be his long-lost brother, who had spent decades in bondage in the Deep South. Another time, he assisted Osborne Anderson, the only African-American member of John Brown's force to survive the Harpers Ferry raid. A businessman as well as an abolitionist, Still supplied coal to the Union Army during the Civil War.

6. Levi Coffin

The Underground Railroad, painted by Charles T. Webber, shows Levi Coffin, his wife Catherine, and Hannah Haydock assisting a group of fugitive slaves.

Bettmann Archive/Getty Images

Known as the "president of the Underground Railroad," Levi Coffin purportedly became an abolitionist at age 7 when he witnessed a column of chained enslaved people being driven to auction. Getting his start bringing food to fugitives hiding out on his family's North Carolina farm, he would grow to be a prosperous merchant and prolific "stationmaster," first in Newport (now Fountain City), Indiana, and then in Cincinnati. All told, he claimed to have assisted about 3,300 enslaved people, saying he and his wife, Catherine, rarely passed a week without hearing a telltale nighttime knock on their side door. Operating openly, Coffin even hosted anti-slavery lectures and abolitionist sewing society meetings, and, like his fellow Quaker Thomas Garrett, remained defiant when dragged into court. "The dictates of humanity came in opposition to the law of the land," he wrote, "and we ignored the law."

7. Elijah Anderson

The Ohio River, which marked the border between slave and free states, was known in abolitionist circles as the River Jordan. For enslaved people on the lam, Madison, Indiana, served as one particularly attractive crossing point, thanks to an Underground Railroad cell set

up there by blacksmith Elijah Anderson and several other members of the town's Black middle class. Light skinned enough to pass for a white slave owner, Anderson took numerous trips into Kentucky, where he purportedly rounded up 20 to 30 enslaved people at a time and whisked them to freedom, sometimes escorting them as far as the Coffins' home in Newport. The work was exceedingly dangerous. A mob of pro-slavery whites ransacked Madison in 1846 and nearly drowned an Underground Railroad operative, after which Anderson fled upriver to Lawrenceburg, Indiana. Continuing his activities, he assisted roughly 800 additional fugitives prior to being jailed in Kentucky for "enticing slaves to run away." On what some sources report to be the very day of his release in 1861, Anderson was suspiciously found dead in his cell.

8. Thaddeus Stevens

American lawyer and legislator Thaddeus Stevens.

Matthew Brady/Bettmann Archive/Getty Images

Pennsylvania congressman Thaddeus Stevens made no secret of his anti-slavery views. A champion of the 14th and 15th amendments, which promised Black citizens equal protection under the law and the right to vote, respectively, he also favored radical reconstruction of the South, including redistribution of land from white plantation owners to former enslaved people. Stevens even paid a spy to infiltrate a group of fugitive slave hunters in his district. It wasn't until 2002, however, when archeologists discovered a secret hiding place in the courtyard of his Lancaster home that his Underground Railroad efforts came to light. "Stationmasters," including author and orator Frederick Douglass and Secretary of State William H. Seward.

 The 1921 "**Tulsa Race Massacre**" in Oklahoma was one of the deadliest events of racist violence in America's history."

"Thirty-five city blocks were burned to the ground and decades of segregation, trauma and financial hardship followed for the Black community. "

For years, the massacre that took place from May 31 to June 1, 1921, was left out of history books and school curriculums. It was underplayed, inaccurately reported or not reported on at all. It began to disappear from libraries and conversations about American history altogether. But one century later, historians, writers, political leaders and community activists are bringing forth discussions that focus on the event, what led up to it and how it's still impacting generations of Americans to this day.

A city once hail as the Black Wall Street was burned down and all the surviving survivors were displaced without any place to live. Many blacks lost their lives and an accurate account isn't known due to the brutalities.

Diane j. Cho the history Behind the 1921 Tulsa Race Massacre

Monday May 31, 2021 @ 7:40 a.m.

https://www.legendsofamerica.com/ah-slaveryglossary

Reference

Answersafrica.com/8-most-horrific-and-inhuman-black-slave-punishment-in-the-history-of-slavery, html

https://listverse.com/2019/10/23/10-of-the-worst-massacres-of-african-americans-disturbing-images/new

"On May 30, 1921, Dick Rowland, an African American who was a shiner was accused of assaulting a white elevator operator, named Sarah Page. And from that lie, the Tribune printed a story that a rape had occurred. There was a confrontation between an armed African

American man that where there to protect Rowland and a white protestor that resulted in a death this ignited the Tulsa massacre."

Over a period of two days, the white mob, looted and burned down this community killing blacks and destroying their community. Airplanes dropped bombs on this striving black community burning it down to the ground.

After the massacre, there was a brief injury but it was swept under the rug, the massacre was absent from our history books until in 1997 when a Tulsa Race Riot Commission was formed by the state of Oklahoma to investigate the massacre. Accounts were taken from the survivors who were still alive and witnessed the massacre.

It is a missed opportunity that the government didn't acknowledge or prosecute the people who were involved in this disgusting act. The Massacre left thousandths of people homeless but, they didn't care because they were blacks.

Those people whom lost everything were not compensated from the government for the Tulsa Oklahoma massacre. Even when they prevented history from acknowledging it earlier, I am happy to say, that this year, 2021, President Biden acknowledged what happen in history. In his speech, President Biden acknowledged all the brave blacks who lost their lives due to a lie. Why was this massacre coved up for years? We know that whites didn't want their children to find out about the disgusting and horrible acts their ancestors did to the African American People.

Martin Luther King Jr.

Martin Luther King Jr. was a scholar and minister who led the civil rights movement. After his assassination, he was memorialized by Martin Luther King Jr. Day.

Who Was Martin Luther King Jr?

Martin Luther King Jr. was a Baptist minister and civil-rights activist who had a seismic impact on race relations in the United States, beginning in the mid-1950s.

Among his many efforts, King headed the Southern Christian Leadership Conference (SCLC). Through his activism and inspirational speeches, he played a pivotal role in ending the legal segregation of African American citizens in the United States, as well as the creation of the Civil Rights Act of 1964 and the Voting Rights Act of 1965.

King won the Nobel Peace Prize in 1964, among several other honors. He continues to be remembered as one of the most influential and inspirational African American leaders in history.

Early Life

Born as Michael King Jr. on January 15, 1929, Martin Luther King Jr. was the middle child of Michael King Sr. and Alberta Williams King.

The King and Williams families had roots in rural Georgia. Martin Jr.'s grandfather, A.D. Williams, was a rural minister for years and then moved to Atlanta in 1893. He took over the small, struggling Ebenezer Baptist church with around 13 members and made it into a forceful congregation. He married Jennie Celeste Parks and they had one child that survived, Alberta. Martin Sr. came from a family of sharecroppers in a poor farming community. He married Alberta in 1926 after an eight-year courtship. The newlyweds moved to A.D.'s home in Atlanta. Martin Sr. stepped in as pastor of Ebenezer Baptist Church upon the death of his father-in-law in 1931. He too became a successful minister and adopted the name Martin Luther King Sr. in honor of the German Protestant religious leader **Martin Luther**. In due time, Michael Jr. would follow his father's lead and adopt the name himself. King had an older sister, Willie Christine, and a younger brother, Alfred Daniel Williams King. The King children grew up in a secure and loving environment. Martin Sr. was more the disciplinarian, while his wife's gentleness easily balanced out the father's strict hand.

Though they undoubtedly tried, King's parents couldn't shield him completely from racism. Martin Sr. fought against racial prejudice, not just because his race suffered, but because he considered racism and segregation to be an affront to God's will. He strongly discouraged any sense of class superiority in his children which left a lasting impression on Martin Jr. Growing up in Atlanta, Georgia, King entered public school at age five. In May 1936 he was baptized, but the event made little impression on him. In May 1941, King was 12 years old when his grandmother, Jennie, died of a heart attack. The event was traumatic for King, more so because he was out watching a parade against his parents' wishes when she died. Distraught at the news, young King jumped from a second-story window at the family home, allegedly attempting suicide. King attended **Booker T. Washington** High School, where he was said to be a precocious student. He skipped both the ninth and eleventh grades, and entered Morehouse College in Atlanta at age 15, in 1944. He was a popular student, especially with his female classmates, but an unmotivated student who floated through his first two years. Although his family was deeply involved in the church and worship, King questioned religion in general and felt uncomfortable with overly emotional displays of religious worship. This discomfort continued through much of his adolescence, initially leading him to decide against entering the ministry, much to his father's dismay. But in his junior year, King took a Bible class, renewed his faith and began to envision a career in the ministry. In the fall of his senior year, he told his father of his decision.

Education and Spiritual Growth

In 1948, King earned a sociology degree from Morehouse College and attended the liberal Crozer Theological Seminary in Chester, Pennsylvania. He thrived in all his studies, and was valedictorian of his class in 1951, and elected student body president. He also earned a fellowship for graduate study.

But King also rebelled against his father's more conservative influence by drinking beer and playing pool while at college. He became involved with a white woman and went through a difficult time before he could break off the affair. During his last year in seminary, King came under the guidance of Morehouse College President Benjamin E. Mays who influenced King's spiritual development. Mays was an outspoken advocate for racial equality and encouraged King to view Christianity as a potential force for social change. After being accepted at several colleges for his doctoral study, King enrolled at Boston University.

During the work on his doctorate, King met Coretta Scott, an aspiring singer and musician at the New England Conservatory school in Boston. They were married in June 1953 and had four children, Yolanda, Martin Luther King III, Dexter Scott and Bernice.

In 1954, while still working on his dissertation, King became pastor of the Dexter Avenue Baptist Church of Montgomery, Alabama. He completed his Ph.D. and earned his degree in 1955. King was only 25 years old.

Montgomery Bus Boycott On March 2, 1955, a 15-year-old girl refused to give up her seat to a white man on a Montgomery city bus in violation of local law. Teenager Claudette Colvin was then arrested and taken to jail. At first, the local chapter of the NAACP felt they had an excellent test case to challenge Montgomery's segregated bus policy. But then it was revealed that Colvin was pregnant and civil rights leaders feared this would scandalize the deeply religious Black community and make Colvin (and, thus the group's efforts) less credible in the eyes of sympathetic white **people.**

On December 1, 1955, they got another chance to make their case. That evening, 42-year-old Rosa Parks boarded the Cleveland Avenue bus to go home after an exhausting day at work. She sat in the first row of the "colored" section in the middle of the bus. As the bus traveled its route, all the seats in the white section filled up, then several more white passengers boarded the bus.

The bus driver noted that there were several white men standing and demanded that Parks and several other African Americans give up their seats. Three other African American passengers reluctantly gave up their places, but Parks remained seated. The driver asked her again to give up her seat and again she refused. Parks was arrested and booked for violating the Montgomery City Code. At her trial a week later, in a 30-minute hearing, Parks was found guilty and fined $10 and assessed $4 court fee. On the night that Parks was arrested, **E.D. Nixon, head of the local NAACP chapter met with King and other local civil rights leaders to plan a Montgomery Bus Boycott. King was elected to lead the boycott** because he was young, well-trained with solid family connections and had professional standing. But he was also new to the community and had few enemies, so it was felt he would have strong credibility with the Black community. In his first speech as the group's president, King declared, "We have no alternative but to protest. For many years we have shown an amazing patience. We have sometimes given our white brothers the feeling that we liked the way we were being treated. But we come here tonight to be saved from that

patience that makes us patient with anything less than freedom and justice."
King's skillful rhetoric put new energy into the civil rights struggle in Alabama. The bus boycott involved 382 days of walking to work, harassment, violence, and intimidation for Montgomery's African American community. Both King's and Nixon's homes were attacked.

But the African American community also took legal action against the city ordinance arguing that it was unconstitutional based on the Supreme Court's "separate is never equal" decision in *Brown v. Board of Education*. After being defeated in several lower court rulings and suffering large financial losses, the city of Montgomery lifted the law mandating segregated public transportation.

Southern Christian Leadership Conference

Flush with victory, African American civil rights leaders recognized the need for a national organization to help coordinate their efforts. In January 1957, King, Ralph Abernathy and 60 ministers and civil rights activists founded the Southern Christian Leadership Conference to harness the moral authority and organizing power of Black churches. They would help conduct non-violent protests to promote civil rights reform.

King's participation in the organization gave him a base of operation throughout the South, as well as a national platform. The organization felt the best place to start to give African Americans a voice was to enfranchise them in the voting process. In February 1958, the SCLC sponsored more than 20 mass meetings in key southern cities to register Black voters in the South. King met with religious and civil rights leaders and lectured all over the country on race-related issues. In 1959, with the help of the American Friends Service Committee, and inspired by Mahatma Gandhi's success with non-violent activism, King visited Gandhi's birthplace in India. The trip affected him in a profound way, increasing his commitment to America's civil rights struggle. African American civil rights activist Bayard Rustin, who had studied Gandhi's teachings, became one of King's associates and counseled him to dedicate himself to the principles of nonviolence. Rustin served as King's mentor and advisor throughout his early activism and was the main organizer of the 1963 March on Washington. But Rustin was also a controversial figure at the time, being a homosexual with alleged ties to the Communist Party. Though his counsel was invaluable to King, many of his other supporters urged him to distance himself from Rustin.

Greensboro Sit-In

In February 1960, a group of African American students in North Carolina began what became known as the Greensboro sit-in movement.

Bad Bunny

(1994–)

The students would sit at racially segregated lunch counters in the city's stores. When asked to leave or sit in the colored section, they just remained seated, subjecting themselves to verbal and sometimes physical abuse.

The movement quickly gained traction in several other cities. In April 1960, the SCLC held a conference at Shaw University in Raleigh, North Carolina with local sit-in leaders. King encouraged students to continue to use nonviolent methods during their protests.

Out of this meeting, **the Student Nonviolent Coordinating Committee** formed and for a time, worked closely with the SCLC. By August of 1960, the sit-ins had been successful in ending segregation at lunch counters in 27 southern cities. By 1960, King was gaining national exposure. He returned to Atlanta to become co-pastor with his father at Ebenezer Baptist Church but also continued his civil rights efforts.

On October 19, 1960, King and 75 students entered a local department store and requested lunch-counter service but were denied. When they refused to leave the counter area, King and 36 others were arrested. Realizing the incident would hurt the city's reputation, Atlanta's mayor negotiated a truce and charges were eventually dropped. But soon after, King was imprisoned for violating his probation on a traffic conviction.

The news of his imprisonment entered the 1960 presidential campaign when candidate **John F. Kennedy** **made a phone call to Coretta** Scott King. Kennedy expressed his concern for King's harsh treatment for the traffic ticket and political pressure was quickly set in motion. King was soon released.

Letter from Birmingham Jail

In the spring of 1963, King organized a demonstration in downtown Birmingham, Alabama. With entire families in attendance, city police turned dogs and fire hoses on demonstrators. King was jailed along with large numbers of his supporters, but the event drew nationwide attention. However, King was personally criticized by Black and white clergy alike for taking risks and endangering the children who attended the demonstration.

In his famous <u>Letter from Birmingham Jail</u>, King eloquently spelled out his theory of non-violence: "Nonviolent direct action seeks to create such a crisis and foster such a tension that a community, which has constantly refused to negotiate, is forced to confront the issue."

'I Have a Dream' Speech

By the end of the Birmingham campaign, King and his supporters were making plans for a massive demonstration on the nation's capital composed of multiple organizations, all asking for peaceful change. On August 28, 1963, the historic **March on Washington drew more than 200,000 people in the** shadow of the Lincoln Memorial. It was here that King made his famous "I Have a Dream" speech, emphasizing his belief that someday all men could be brothers

"I have a dream that my four children will one day live in a nation where they will not be judged by the color of their skin but by the content of their character." **— Martin Luther King, Jr. / "I Have a Dream" speech, August 28, 1963**

The rising tide of civil rights agitation produced a strong effect on public opinion. Many people in cities not experiencing racial tension began to question the nation's Jim Crow laws and the near-century of second-class treatment of African American citizens.

Nobel Peace Prize

This resulted in the passage of the <u>Civil Rights Act of 1964</u>, **authorizing the federal government to enforce** desegregation of public accommodations and outlawing discrimination in publicly owned facilities. This also led to King receiving the Nobel Peace Prize in 1964.

King's struggle continued throughout the 1960s. Often, it seemed as though the pattern of progress was two steps forward and one step back. On March 7, 1965, a civil rights march, planned from Selma to Montgomery, Alabama's capital, turned violent as police with nightsticks and tear gas met the demonstrators as they tried to cross the Edmund Pettus Bridge.

King was not in the march; however, the attack was televised showing horrifying images of marchers being bloodied and severely injured.

Seventeen demonstrators were hospitalized in a day that would be called "<u>Bloody Sunday</u>."

A second march was canceled due to a restraining order to prevent the march from taking place. A third march was planned and this time King made sure he was part of it. Not wanting to alienate southern judges by violating the restraining order, a different approach was taken. On March 9, 1965, a procession of 2,500 marchers, both Black and white, set out once again to cross the Pettus Bridge and confronted barricades and state troopers. Instead of forcing a confrontation, King led his followers to kneel in prayer and they then turned back.

Alabama governor **George Wallace continued to try to prevent another march until President Lyndon B. Johnson pledged his support and ordered U.S.** Army troops and the Alabama National Guard to protect the protestors. On March 21, approximately 2,000 people began **a march from Selma to Montgomery, the state capitol. On March 25, the number of marchers, which had** grown to an estimated 25,000, gathered in front of the state capitol where King delivered a televised speech. Five months after the historic peaceful protest, President Johnson signed the 1965 Voting Rights Act. From late 1965 through 1967, King expanded his civil rights efforts into other larger American cities, including Chicago and Los Angeles. But he met with increasing criticism and public challenges from young Black power leaders. King's patient, non-violent approach and appeal to white middle-class citizens alienated many Black militants who considered his methods too weak, too late and ineffective. To address this criticism, King began making a link between discrimination and poverty, and he began to speak out against the **Vietnam War**. He felt that America's involvement in Vietnam was politically untenable and the government's conduct in the war discriminatory to the poor. He sought to broaden his base by forming a multi-racial coalition to address the economic and unemployment problems of all disadvantaged people.

Who Killed Martin Luther King Jr.?

By 1968, the years of demonstrations and confrontations were beginning to wear on King. He had grown tired of marches, going to jail, and living under the constant threat of death. He was becoming discouraged at the slow progress of civil rights in America and the increasing criticism from other African American leaders.

Plans were in the works for another march on Washington to revive his movement and bring attention to a widening range of issues. In the spring of 1968, a labor strike by Memphis sanitation workers drew King to one last crusade. On April 3, he gave his final and what proved to be an eerily prophetic speech, "I've Been to the Mountaintop," in which he told supporters at the Mason Temple in Memphis, "I've seen the promised land. I may not get there with you. But I want you to know tonight that we, as a people, will get to the Promised Land." The next day, while standing on a balcony outside his room at the Lorraine Motel, Martin Luther King Jr. was killed by a sniper's bullet. The shooter, a malcontent drifter and former convict named James Earl Ray, was eventually apprehended after a two-month, international manhunt. The assassination sparked riots and demonstrations in more than 100 cities across the country. In 1969, Ray pleaded guilty to assassinating King and was sentenced to 99 years in prison. He died in prison on April 23, 1998.

King's life had a seismic impact on race relations in the United States. Years after his death, he is the most widely known African American leader of his era. His life and work have been honored with a national holiday, schools and public buildings named after him, and a memorial on Independence Mall in Washington, D.C.

But his life remains controversial as well. In the 1970s, FBI files, released under the Freedom of Information Act, revealed that he was under government surveillance, and suggested his involvement in adulterous relationships and communist influences.

Over the years, extensive archival studies have led to a more balanced and comprehensive assessment of his life, portraying him as a complex figure: flawed, fallible and limited in his control over the mass movements with which he was associated, yet a visionary leader who was deeply committed to achieving social justice through nonviolent means.

Martin Luther King Jr. Day

In 1983, **President Ronald Reagan** signed into law a bill creating Martin Luther King Jr. Day, a federal holiday honoring the legacy of the slain civil rights leader.

Martin Luther King Jr. Day was first celebrated in 1986, and in all 50 states in 2000.

Citation Information

Article Title

Martin Luther King Jr. Biography

Author

Biography.com Editors

Website Name
The Biography.com website
URL
https://www.biography.com/activist/martin-luther-king-jr
Access Date
September 29, 2021
Publisher
A&E Television Networks
Last Updated
January 13, 2021, original published date April 2, 2014

Rosa Parks, née **Rosa Louise McCauley**,

(born February 4, 1913, Tuskegee, Alabama, U.S.—died October 24, 2005, Detroit, Michigan), American civil rights activist whose refusal to relinquish her seat on a public bus precipitated the 1955–56 Montgomery bus boycott in Alabama, which became the spark that ignited the civil rights movement in the United States.

Born to parents James McCauley, a skilled stonemason and carpenter, and Leona Edwards McCauley, a teacher, in Tuskegee, Alabama, Rosa Louise McCauley spent much of her childhood and youth ill with chronic tonsillitis. When she was two years old,

shortly after the birth of her younger brother, Sylvester, her parents chose to separate. Estranged from their father from then on, the children moved with their mother to live on their maternal grandparents' farm in Pine Level, Alabama, outside Montgomery. The children's great-grandfather, a former indentured
  servant, also lived there; he died when Rosa was six. For much of her childhood, Rosa was educated at home by her mother, who also worked as a teacher at a nearby school. Rosa helped with chores on the farm and learned to cook and sew. Farm life, though, was less than idyllic. The Ku Klux Klan was a constant threat, as she later recalled, "burning Negro churches, schools, flogging and killing" Black families. Rosa's grandfather would often keep watch at night, rifle in hand, awaiting a mob of violent white men. The house's windows and doors were boarded shut with the family, frequently joined by Rosa's widowed aunt and her five children, inside. On nights thought to be especially dangerous, the children would have to go to bed with their clothes on so that they would be ready if the family needed to escape. Sometimes Rosa would choose to stay awake and keep watch with her grandfather.

Rosa and her family experienced <u>racism</u> in less violent ways, too. When Rosa entered school in Pine Level, she had to attend a <u>segregated</u> establishment where one teacher was put in charge of about 50 or 60 schoolchildren. Though white children in the area were bused to their schools, Black children had to walk. Public transportation, drinking fountains, restaurants, and schools were all segregated under <u>Jim Crow laws</u>. At age 11 Rosa entered the Montgomery Industrial School for Girls, where Black girls were taught regular school subjects alongside domestic skills. She went on to attend a Black <u>junior high school</u> for 9th grade and a Black teacher's college for 10th and part of 11th grade. At age 16, however, she was forced to leave school because of an illness in the family, and she began cleaning the houses of white people. In 1932, at age 19, Rosa married Raymond Parks, a barber and a civil rights activist, who encouraged her to return to <u>high school</u> and earn a diploma. She later made a living as a seamstress. In 1943 Rosa Parks became a member of the Montgomery chapter of the <u>National Association for the Advancement of Colored People</u> (NAACP), and she served as its secretary until 1956.

On December 1, 1955, Parks was riding a crowded Montgomery city bus when the driver,

upon noticing that there were white passengers standing in the aisle, asked Parks and other
Black passengers to surrender their seats and stand. Three of the passengers left their seats, but Parks refused. She was subsequently arrested and fined $10 for the offense and $4 for court costs, neither of which she paid. Instead, she accepted Montgomery NAACP chapter President E.D. Nixon's offer to help her appeal the conviction and thus challenge legal segregation in Alabama. Both Parks and Nixon knew that they were opening themselves to harassment and death threats, but they also knew that the case had the potential to spark national outrage. Under the aegis of the Montgomery Improvement Association—led by the young pastor of the Dexter Avenue Baptist Church, Martin Luther King, Jr.—a boycott of the municipal bus company began on December 5. African Americans constituted some 70 percent of the ridership, and the absence of their bus fares cut deeply into revenue. The boycott lasted 381 days, and even people outside Montgomery embraced the cause: protests of
segregated restaurants, pools, and other public facilities took place all over the United States. On November 13, 1956, the U.S. Supreme Court upheld a lower court's decision declaring Montgomery's segregated bus seating

unconstitutional, and a court
order to integrate the buses was served on
December 20; the boycott ended the following
day. For her role in igniting the successful
campaign, Parks became known as the "mother
of the civil rights movement."

Simplifications of Parks's story claimed that
she had refused to give up her bus seat because
she was tired rather than because she was
protesting unfair treatment. But she was an
accomplished activist by the time of her arrest,
having worked with the NAACP on other civil
rights cases, such as that of the Scottsboro Boys,
nine Black youths falsely accused of sexually
assaulting two white women. According to
Parks's autobiography, "I was not tired
physically, or no more tired than I usually was at
the end of a working day. I was not old, although
some people have an image of me as being old
then. I was 42. No, the only tired I was, was tired
of giving in." Parks was not the first Black
woman to refuse to give up her bus seat for a
white person—15-year-old Claudette Colvin had
been arrested for the same offense nine months
earlier, and dozens of other Black women had
preceded them in the history of segregated public
transit. However, as secretary of the local
NAACP, and with the Montgomery
Improvement Association behind her, Parks had

access to resources and publicity that those other women had not had. It was her case that forced the city of Montgomery to desegregate city buses permanently. In 1957 Parks moved with her husband and mother to Detroit, where from 1965 to 1988 she worked on the staff of Michigan Congressman John Conyers, Jr. She remained active in the NAACP, and the Southern Christian Leadership Conference established an annual Rosa Parks Freedom Award in her honour. In 1987 she cofounded the Rosa and Raymond Parks Institute for Self-Development to provide career training for young people and offer teenagers the opportunity to learn about the history of the civil rights movement. She received numerous awards, including the Presidential Medal of Freedom (1996) and the Congressional Gold Medal (1999). Her autobiography, *Rosa Parks: My Story* (1992), was written with Jim Haskins.

Though achieving the desegregation of Montgomery's city buses was an incredible feat, Parks was not satisfied with that victory. She saw that the United States was still failing to respect and protect the lives of Black Americans. Martin Luther King, Jr., who had been brought to national attention by his organization of the Montgomery bus boycott, was assassinated less than a decade after Parks's case was won.

Biographer Kathleen Tracy noted that Parks, in one of her last interviews, would not quite say that she was happy: "I do the very best I can to look upon life with optimism and hope and looking forward to a better day, but I don't think there is any such thing as complete happiness. It pains me that there is still a lot of Klan activity and racism. I think when you say you're happy, you have everything that you need and everything that you want, and nothing more to wish for. I haven't reached that stage yet."

After Parks died in 2005, her body lay in state in the rotunda of the U.S. Capitol, an honor reserved for private citizens who performed a great service for their country. For two days mourners visited her casket and gave thanks for her dedication to civil rights. Parks was the first woman and only the second Black person to receive the distinction.

December 1, 1955, in which Rosa Parks, an African American woman, had refused to surrender her bus seat to a white passenger and as a consequence was arrested for violating the city's segregation law. Activists formed the Montgomery Improvement Association to boycott the transit system and chose King as their...

Montgomery bus boycott, mass protest against the bus system of Montgomery, Alabama, by civil rights activists and their supporters that led to a 1956 U.S. Supreme Court decision declaring that Montgomery's buses were unconstitutional. The 381-day bus boycott also brought the Rev. Martin Luther King, Jr., into the spotlight as one of the most important leaders of the American civil rights movement.

The event that triggered the boycott took place in Montgomery on December 1, 1955, after seamstress Rosa Parks refused to give her seat to a white passenger on a city bus. Local laws dictated that African American passengers sat at the back of the bus while whites sat in front. If the white section became full, African Americans had to give up their seats in the back. When Parks refused to move to give her seat to a white rider, she was taken to jail; she was later bailed out by a local civil rights leader.

Many of Montgomery's African American residents were politically organized long before Parks was arrested. For example, the Women's Political Council (WPC) was founded in 1946, and it had been lobbying the city for improved conditions on the buses for a decade before the bus boycott began. In addition, Montgomery had an active branch of the National Association for the Advancement of Colored People (NAACP), where Parks also worked as a secretary.

Although Parks was not the first resident of Montgomery to refuse to give up her seat to a white passenger, local civil rights leaders decided to capitalize on her arrest as a chance to challenge local segregation laws. Shortly after Parks's arrest, Jo Ann Robinson, a leader of the WPC, and E.D. Nixon, president of the local NAACP, printed and distributed leaflets describing Parks's arrest and called for a one-day boycott of the city buses on December 5. They believed that the boycott could be effective because the Montgomery bus system was heavily dependent on African American riders, who made up about 75 percent of the ridership. Some 90 percent of the African American residents stayed off the buses that day.

The boycott was so successful that local civil rights leaders decided to extend it indefinitely. A group of local ministers formed the Montgomery Improvement Association (MIA) to support and sustain the boycott and the legal challenge to the segregation laws. Martin Luther King, the charismatic young pastor of the Dexter Avenue Baptist Church, was elected president of the MIA. A powerful orator, he was new to the area and had few enemies, and, thus, local leaders believed he could rally the various factions of the African American community to the cause. The MIA initially asked for first-come, first-served seating, with African Americans starting in the rear and white passengers beginning in the front of the bus. They also asked that African American bus drivers be hired for routes primarily made up of African American riders. The bus companies and Montgomery officials refused to meet those demands. Many white citizens retaliated against the African American community: King's home was bombed, and many boycotters were threatened or fired from their jobs. Several times the police arrested protesters and took them to jail, once charging 80 leaders of the boycott with violating a 1921 law that barred conspiracies to interfere with lawful business without just cause.

Despite such intimidation, the boycott continued for more than a year. The MIA filed a federal suit against bus segregation, and on June 5, 1956, a federal district court declared segregated seating on buses to be unconstitutional. The Supreme Court upheld that ruling in mid-November. The federal decision went into effect on December 20, 1956.

The boycott garnered a great deal of publicity in the national press, and King became well known throughout the country.

https://www.britannica.com/biography/R

Malcolm X

Biography
May 19, 1925 to February 21, 1965
As the nation's most visible proponent of **Black Nationalism**, Malcolm X's challenge to the multiracial, nonviolent approach of Martin Luther King, Jr., helped set the tone for the ideological and tactical conflicts that took place within the black freedom struggle of the 1960s. Given Malcolm X's abrasive criticism of King and his advocacy of racial separatism, it is not surprising that King rejected the occasional overtures from one of his fiercest critics. However, after Malcolm's assassination in 1965, King wrote to his widow, Betty Shabazz: "While we did not always see eye to eye on methods to solve the race problem, I always had a deep affection for Malcolm and felt that he had the great ability to put his finger on the existence and root of the problem" (King, 26 February 1965).

Malcolm little was born to Louise and Earl Little in Omaha, Nebraska, on 19 May 1925. His father died when he was six years old—the victim, he believed, of a white racist group. Following his father's death, Malcolm recalled, "Some kind of psychological deterioration hit our family circle and began to eat away our pride" (Malcolm X, *Autobiography*, 14). By the end of the 1930s Malcolm's mother had been

Institutionalized, and he became a ward of the court to be raised by white guardians in various reform schools and foster homes.

Malcolm joined the Nation of Islam (NOI) while serving a prison term in Massachusetts on burglary charges. Shortly after his release in 1952, he moved to Chicago and became a minister under Elijah Muhammad, abandoning his "slave name," and becoming Malcolm X (Malcolm X, "We Are Rising"). By the late 1950s, Malcolm had become the NOI's leading spokesman.

Although Malcolm rejected King's message of **nonviolence**, he respected King as a "fellow-leader of our people," sending King NOI articles as early as 1957 and inviting him to participate in mass meetings throughout the early 1960s (*Papers* 5:491). Although Malcolm was particularly interested that King hear Elijah

Muhammad's message, he also sought to create an open forum for black leaders to explore solutions to the "race problem" (Malcolm X, 31 July 1963). King never accepted Malcolm's invitations, however, leaving communication with him to his secretary, Maude **Ballou**.

Despite his repeated overtures to King, Malcolm did not refrain from criticizing him publicly. "The only revolution in which the goal is loving your enemy," Malcolm told an audience in 1963, "is the Negro revolution … That's no revolution" (Malcolm X, "Message to the Grassroots," 9).

In the spring of 1964, Malcolm broke away from the NOI and made a pilgrimage to Mecca. When he returned, he began following a course that paralleled King's—combining religious leadership and political action. Although King told reporters that Malcolm's separation from Elijah Muhammad "holds no particular significance to the present civil rights efforts," he argued that if "tangible gains are not made soon all across the country, we must honestly face the prospect that some Negroes might be tempted to accept some oblique path [such] as that Malcolm X proposes" (King, 16 March 1964).

Ten days later, during the Senate debate on the **Civil Rights Act of 1964**, King and Malcolm met for the first and only time. After holding a press conference in the Capitol on the proceedings, King encountered Malcolm in the hallway. As King recalled in a 3 April letter, "At the end of the conference, he came and spoke to me, and I readily shook his hand." King defended shaking the hand of an adversary by saying that "my position is that of kindness and reconciliation" (King, 3 April 1965).

Malcolm's primary concern during the remainder of 1964 was to establish ties with the black activists he saw as more militant than King. He met with a number of workers from the **Student Nonviolent Coordinating Committee** (SNCC), including SNCC chairman John **Lewis** and Mississippi organizer Fannie Lou **Hamer**. Malcolm saw his newly created Organization of African American Unity (OAAU) as a potential source of ideological guidance for the more militant veterans of the southern civil rights movement. At the same time, he looked to the southern struggle for inspiration in his effort to revitalize the Black Nationalist movement.

In January 1965, he revealed in an interview that the OAAU would "support fully and without compromise any action by any group that is designed to get meaningful immediate results" (Malcolm X, *Two Speeches*, 31). Malcolm urged civil rights groups to unite, telling a gathering at a symposium sponsored by the **Congress of Racial Equality**: "We want freedom now, but we're not going to get it saying 'We Shall Overcome.' We've got to fight to overcome" (Malcolm X, *Malcolm X Speaks*, 38). In early 1965, while King was jailed in Selma, Alabama, Malcolm traveled to Selma, where he had a private meeting with Coretta

Scott **King**. "I didn't come to Selma to make his job difficult," he assured Coretta. "I really did come thinking that I could make it easier. If the white people realize what the alternative is, perhaps they will be more willing to hear Dr. King" (Scott King, 256).

On 21 February 1965, just a few weeks after his visit to Selma, Malcolm X was assassinated. King called his murder a "great tragedy" and expressed his regret that it "occurred at a time when Malcolm X was … moving toward a greater understanding of the nonviolent movement" (King, 24 February 1965). He asserted that Malcolm's murder deprived "the world of a potentially great leader" (King, "The Nightmare of Violence"). Malcolm's death signaled the beginning of bitter battles involving proponents of the ideological alternatives the two men represented.

Malcolm X, Interview by Harry Ring over Station WBAI-FM in New York, in *Two Speeches by Malcolm X*, 1965.

https://kinginstitute.stanford.edu/encycloped ia/malcolm-x

President Barack Obama

Barack Obama is the 44th President of the United States. His story is the American story -- values from the heartland, a middle-class upbringing in a strong family, hard work and education as the means of getting ahead, and the conviction that a life so blessed should be lived in service to others.

Barack H. Obama is the 44th President of the United States.

His story is the American story — values from the heartland, a middle-class upbringing in a strong family, hard work and education as the means of getting ahead, and the conviction that a life so blessed should be lived in service to others. With a father from Kenya and a mother from Kansas, President Obama was born in Hawaii on August 4, 1961. He was raised with help from his grandfather, who served in Patton's army, and his grandmother, who worked her way up from the secretarial pool to middle management at a bank. After working his way through college with the help of scholarships and student loans, President Obama moved to Chicago, where he worked with a group of churches to help rebuild communities devastated by the closure of local steel plants.

He went on to attend law school, where he became the first African-American president of the *Harvard Law Review*. Upon graduation, he returned to Chicago to help lead a voter registration drive, teach constitutional law at the University of Chicago, and remain active in his community. President Obama's years of public service are based around his unwavering belief in the ability to unite people around a politics of purpose. In the Illinois State Senate, he passed the first major ethics reform in 25 years, cut taxes for working families, and expanded health care for children and their parents. As a United States Senator, he reached across the aisle to pass groundbreaking lobbying reform, lock up the world's most dangerous weapons, and bring transparency to government by putting federal spending online.

He was elected the 44th President of the United States on November 4, 2008, and sworn in on January 20, 2009. After being re-elected in 2012, President Obama is currently serving his second and final term, which will end in January 2017.

President Obama and his wife, Michelle, are the proud parents of two daughters, Malia and Sasha.

https://obamawhitehouse.archives.gov/admi nistration/president-obama

No matter how and what tactics they've used to try to hold us back as a race, we have prevailed. I mourned when President Barack Obama was elected; he was the first African American President. He had his share of road blocks placed in his path but, he maneuvered his way and created a common ground for all of us to strive.

Martin Luther King Jr., Malcom X and the 44th President of the United States, President Obama, these men had a huge impact of the world; they paved the way for more trailblazers. Their self-s sacrificing efforts have opened the doors that were shut because these courageous men refused to be silenced even if it meant losing their lives.

The New York Times

MINNEAPOLIS — The killing of George Floyd on a Minneapolis corner led to nationwide protests, a reckoning over racial injustice touching on virtually every aspect of American life and, on Friday, a substantial prison sentence — 22 and a half years — for the former police officer, Derek Chauvin, who ignored Mr. Floyd's desperate cries for help and pressed his knee into Mr. Floyd's neck for what seemed an eternity.

The sentence was less than the 30 years prosecutors had sought, but far more than the penalty that lawyers for Mr. Chauvin, 45, had requested: probation and the time he has already spent behind bars. The sentence means the earliest Mr. Chauvin could be eligible for release on parole, experts said, would be in 2035 or 2036, when he is close to 60 years old.

In delivering Mr. Chauvin's sentence on Friday, Judge Peter A. Cahill referred to the "particular cruelty" of the crime, which was captured in a widely shared cellphone video, as Mr. Chauvin held Mr. Floyd down for more than nine minutes in May 2020. Mr. Floyd could be heard crying out more than 20 times that he could not breathe.

Shortly after reading the sentence from the bench, Judge Cahill issued a 22-page memorandum about his decision, writing, "Part of the mission of the Minneapolis Police Department is to give citizens 'voice and respect.'" But Mr. Chauvin, the judge wrote, had instead "treated Mr. Floyd without respect and denied him the dignity owed to all human beings and which he certainly would have extended to a friend or neighbor."

Another article about the sentencing of Derek Chauvin
Judge sentences Derek Chauvin to over 22 years for murder of George Floyd

Crystal Hill
·Reporter
Fri, June 25, 2021

Former Minneapolis Police Officer Derek Chauvin was sentenced Friday to 22 and a half years in prison for the murder of George Floyd, more than one year after Floyd's death sparked an international movement against police brutality. Hennepin County Judge Peter Cahill, who presided over Chauvin's murder trial, handed down a sentence of 270 months for charges of second-degree unintentional murder, third-degree murder and second-degree manslaughter in Floyd's May 25, 2020, death. Chauvin received a credit of 199 days served in prison. A jury convicted him of the charges on April 20.

"What the sentence is not based on is emotion or sympathy," Cahill said. "But at the same time, I want to acknowledge the deep and tremendous pain that all the families are feeling, especially the Floyd family. I'm not going to attempt to be profound or clever because it's not the appropriate time. I'm not basing my sentence on public opinion. I'm not basing it on any attempt to send any messages."

Wage gap between blacks and whites is worst in nearly 40 years

by Tanzania Vega   @CNNMoneySeptember 20, 2016: 5:07 AM ET

The wage gap between blacks and whites is the worst it's been in nearly four decades, according to a new report from the Economic Policy Institute.

Last year, the hourly pay gap between blacks and whites widened to 26.7%, with whites making an average of $25.22 an hour compared to $18.49 for blacks, the EPI found. Almost 40 years ago, in 1979, the wage gap between blacks and whites was 18.1%, with whites earning an inflation-adjusted average of $19.62 an hour and blacks earning $16.07 an hour.

What's driving the wage gap has little to do with access to education, disparities in work experience or where someone lives, EPI found. Rather, the researchers found "discrimination...and growing earnings inequality in general," to be the primary factors at play.

"Race is not a skill or characteristic that should have any market value as it relates to your wages, but it does," said Valerie Wilson, the director of the program on Race, Ethnicity and the Economy at the EPI and a co-author of the report.

Related: Milwaukee's staggering black-white divide

Studies have shown that applicants with "black sounding names" like Jamal are less likely to get a call back than applicants with names that appear white. Wilson also cited the skyrocketing incarceration rates of thousands of black men and women in the 1980s and 1990s who were pulled out of the workforce and have since struggled to get back in.

Wage inequities also build up over time, Wilson said. If a black person started working in the 1980s and earned less than a white person, then "that disadvantage carries over."

The researchers found that in 2015 the wage gap between black men with 11 to 20 years of work experience and their white counterparts was wider (23.5%) than it was for black men who had 10 years of experience or less and their white peers (18.7%). Black women with 11 to 20 years of experience were paid 12.6% less than white women with the same experience and those with 10 years' experience or less made 10.8% less.

THE BRONZE PLANTATION AND MR. ED

The growing wage gap between black and white workers

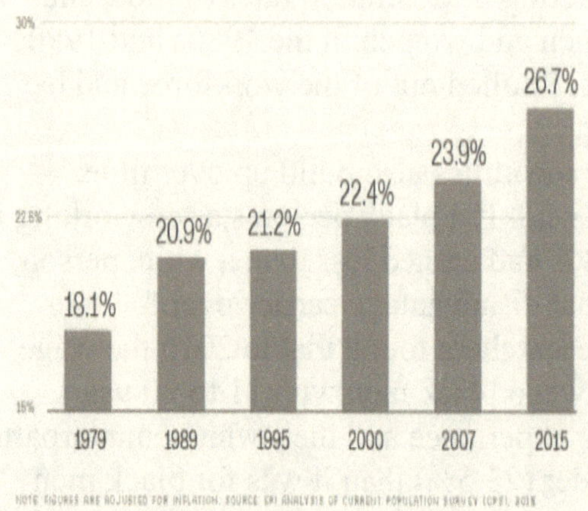

In an effort to combat this type of wage
disparity, Massachusetts lawmakers recently
passed a bill barring employer from asking about

an applicant's previous salary. On a national
level, the Obama administration **announced a
proposal** in February to track wage data by
gender and race for public companies and federal

186

contractors that employ 100 employees or more to help "deliver on the promise of equal pay." Attaining a higher education also failed to close the gap between black and white workers, the report found. Black men with a bachelor's degree or more and who had 11 to 20 years of work experience made 27.2% less than whites with the same level of education and experience. Black women with a bachelor's degree or more and 11 to 20 years of work experience were paid 10.6% less than white women.

Related: Blacks will take hundreds of years to catch up to white wealth

Recent college graduates with less than ten years of work experience also saw gaps in earnings by race. Black women with a bachelor's degree alone were paid 10.7% less than white women, while black men with the same credentials were paid 18% less than their white counterparts.

The wage gap between blacks and whites has ebbed and flowed over the past four decades.

In the 1980s, Wilson said a combination of factors including a stagnant minimum wage (the federal minimum wage was $3.35 an hour between 1981 and 1989), a tough post-recession job market, declining participation in unions and the easing of enforcement on policies, like affirmative action, expanded the gap.

In the 1990s, things started to shift. The minimum wage increased from $3.80 in 1990 to $5.15 in 1997 and there were more jobs and more political support for the enforcement of anti-discrimination laws. "The balance of power shifted to the workers," she said. "People were eager to hire people. Back then almost everyone had a job," she said. But by 2000, the wage gap started growing again. From 2000 to 2007, the gap between whites and black wages increased by 6.3% to 23.9%, driven mostly by stagnant wages, unemployment and slow economic growth, Wilson said. And from 2007, the start of the Great Recession, to 2015 it grew by 10.5%.

Long term, the racial wage gap will ultimately result in less consumer spending, increased poverty and more strain on social safety net programs Wilson said. It can also affect the way people see the American Dream. "You're supposed to come to this country, work hard and do what you need to do to get ahead, but everybody doesn't face that reality."

CNNMoney (New York) first published September 20, 2016: 5:07 AM ET

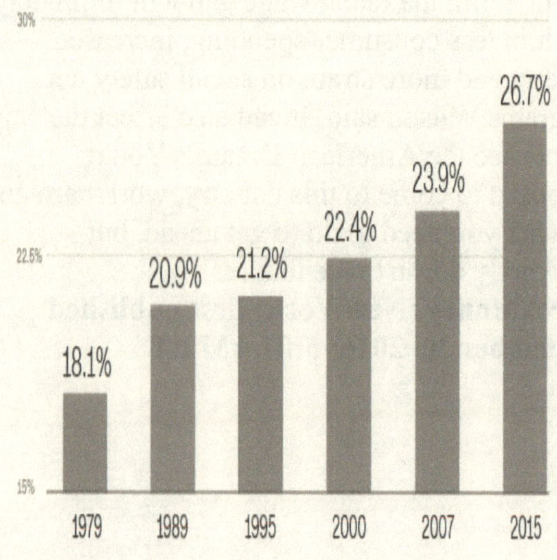

The growing wage gap between black and white workers
30%
26.7%
23.9%
22.4%
22.5%
20.9%
21.2%
18.1%
15%
1979
1989
1995
2000
2007
2015
NOTE: FIGURES ARE ADJUSTED FOR INFLATION. SOURCE: EPI ANALYSIS OF CURRENT POPULATION SURVEY (CPS), 2015

Check out these sites!

**https://money.cnn.com/2016/09/20/news/econ
omy/black-white-wage-gap/index.html**
https://www.yahoo.com/entertainment/history-
behind-1921-tulsa-race-114000338.html
https://www.nps.gov/subjects/undergroundrailr
oad/language-of-slavery.htm

https://www.yahoo.com/entertainment/history-
behind-1921-tulsa-race-114000338.html
**https://blackexcellence.com/black-gospel-
songs/**

**https://www.thepatriot.co.zw/old_posts/sexu
al-abuse-of-black-women-during-slavery-in-
america/**

**After slavery, the author included some
information for the readers emancipation.**
https://www.khanacademy.org/humanities/us-
history/civil-war-era/reconstruction/a/life-after-
slavery

https://make-it-plain.org/2019/03/15/beware-
the-uncle-tom/
https://classicruby.com/2014/02/19/oreo-the-
modern-day-uncle-tom-part-1/

https://www.khanacademy.org/humanities/us-history/civil-war-era/reconstruction/a/life-after-slavery
BY **OLIVIA B. WAXMAN**

AUGUST 20, 2019 12:53 PM EDT
https://time.com/5653369/august-1619-jamestown-history/

https://www.gradesaver.com/narrative-of-the-life-of-frederick-douglass-an-american-slave-written-by-himself/study-guide/quotes

https://en.wikipedia.org/wiki/Slavery_in_the_United_States
https://www.history.com/news/8-key-contributors-to-the-underground-railroad
https://www.nytimes.com/2021/06/25/us/derek-chauvin-22-and-a-half-years-george-floyd.html

https://news.yahoo.com/judge-sentences-derek-chauvin-to-22-years-for-murder-of-george-floyd-200220808.htmlIn

https://www.womenshistory.org/education-resources/biographies/harriet-tub

https://stock.adobe.com/search/images?load_ty pe=search&native_visual_search=&similar_cont e

nt_id=&is_recent_search=&search_type=userty ped&k=slaves

https://www.womenshistory.org/education-resources/biographies/stacey-abrams

free royalty free slave pictures - Bing images

free image of slaves - Bing images

Harriet Tubman

Known as the "Moses of her people," Harriet
Tubman was enslaved, escaped, and helped
others gain their freedom as a "conductor" of the
Underground Railroad. Tubman also served as a
scout, spy, guerrilla soldier, and nurse for the
Union Army during the **Civil War**. She is
considered the first African American woman to

serve in the military. Tubman's exact birth date is unknown, but estimates place it between 1820 and 1822 in Dorchester County, Maryland. Born Araminta Ross, the daughter of Harriet Green and Benjamin Ross, Tubman had eight siblings. By age five, Tubman's owners rented her out to neighbors as a domestic servant. Early signs of her resistance to slavery and its abuses came at age twelve when she intervened to keep her master from beating an enslaved man who tried to escape. She was hit in the head with a two-pound weight, leaving her with a lifetime of severe headaches and narcolepsy. Although slaves were not legally allowed to marry, Tubman entered a marital union with John Tubman, a free black man, in 1844. She took his name and dubbed herself Harriet. Contrary to legend, Tubman did not create the Underground Railroad; it was established in the late eighteenth century by black and white abolitionists. Tubman likely benefitted from this network of escape routes and safe houses in 1849, when she and two brothers escaped north. Her husband refused to join her, and by 1851 he had married a free black woman. Tubman returned to the South several times and helped dozens of people escape. Her success led slaveowners to post a $40,000 reward for her capture or death. Tubman was never caught and never lost a "passenger."

She participated in other antislavery efforts, including supporting John Brown in his failed 1859 raid on the Harpers Ferry, Virginia arsenal.

Through the Underground Railroad, Tubman learned the towns and transportation routes characterizing the South—information that made her important to Union military commanders during the Civil War. As a Union spy and scout, Tubman often transformed herself into an aging woman. She would wander the streets under Confederate control and learn from the enslaved population about Confederate troop placements and supply lines. Tubman helped many of these individuals find food, shelter, and even jobs in the North. She also became a respected guerrilla operative. As a **nurse**, Tubman dispensed herbal remedies to black and white soldiers dying from infection and disease.

After the war, Tubman raised funds to aid freedmen, joined **Elizabeth Cady Stanton** and **Susan B. Anthony** in their quest for women's suffrage, cared for her aging parents, and worked with white writer Sarah

The author selected these famous people to highlight their roles in history and how they helped pathed the way. These men and women gave effortfully and devoted their lives to causes that the privileged take for granted such as, the freedom to live in a world free from oppression.

Glory is one of the best songs ever wrote by John Legend and Common.
It tells our struggles.

One day, when the glory comes
It will be ours, it will be ours
Oh, one day, when the war is won
We will be sure, we will be here sure
Oh, glory, glory
Oh, glory, glory
Hands to the Heavens, no man, no weapon
Formed against, yes glory is destined
Every day women and men become legends
Sins that go against our skin become blessings
The movement is a rhythm to us
Freedom is like religion to us
Justice is juxtaposition in us
Justice for all just ain't specific enough
One son died, his spirit is revisitin' us
Truant livin' livin' in us, resistance is us
That's why Rosa sat on the bus
That's why we walk through Ferguson with our hands up

THE BRONZE PLANTATION AND MR. ED

When it go down we woman and man up
They say, "Stay down" and we stand up
Shots, we on the ground, the camera panned up
King pointed to the mountain top and we ran up
One day, when the glory comes
It will be ours, it will be ours
Oh, one day, when the war is won
We will be sure, we will be here sure
Oh, glory, glory
Oh, glory, glory glory
Now the war is not over
Victory isn't won
And we'll fight on to the finish
Then when it's all done
We'll cry glory, oh glory
We'll cry glory, oh glory
Selma's now for every man, woman and child
Even Jesus got his crown in front of a crowd
They marched with the torch, we gon' run with it
now
Never look back, we done gone hundreds of miles
From dark roads he rose, to become a hero
Facin' the league of justice, his power was the
  people
Enemy is lethal, a king became regal
Saw the face of Jim Crow under a bald eagle
The biggest weapon is to stay peaceful
We sing, our music is the cuts that we bleed
through
Somewhere in the dream we had an epiphany
Now we right the wrongs in history
No one can win the war individually

THE BRONZE PLANTATION AND MR. ED

It takes the wisdom of the elders and young
people's energy
Welcome to the story we call victory
Comin' of the Lord, my eyes have seen the glory
One day, when the glory comes
It will be ours, it will be ours
Oh, one day, when the war is won
We will be sure, we will be here sure
Oh, glory, glory
Oh, glory, glory glory
When the war is done, when it's all said and done
We'll cry glory, oh glory

Must Read!

Slavery by Booker T. Washington
Twelve Years a Slave by Solomon Northup
Narrative of the Life of Frederick
Douglass an   American Slave

Before completion of this book, there was another senseless killing of an unarmed Black by whites while he was jogging.

Brunswick, Georgia (CNN) A jury Wednesday found three White men charged in the killing of Ahmaud Arbery, a 25-year-old Black man, guilty on multiple murder counts, as well as other charges.

The verdict, delivered by nine White women, two White men and one Black man, came after more than 11 hours of deliberation spanning two days. It

followed eight days of testimony, involving 23 witnesses.

Arbery's parents appeared alongside civil rights stalwarts outside the courthouse following the verdict. They praised the prosecution and supporters who joined the family in the fight for justice for their son, whose killing spurred national outrage and helped cast a spotlight on other racially driven crimes around the country.

https://www.cnn.com/2021/11/24/us/ahmaud -arbery-killing-trial-wednesday-jury- deliberations/index.html

{INDIVIDUAL LIFE STORIES}

Living in America while being Black
The author petitioned some friends to voice their views about their experienced being Black in America. Also, she wanted to know their thoughts on the Insurrection that occurred January 6, 2021, incited by Trump. These comments are solely the thoughts of the people who participated in writing down their thoughts on paper. They used the author's book as a platform to voice their concerns.

Also, the author would like to thank them for their wisdom and insight.

Earnest Jenkins

Being a person of color, this is a good thing, as well as a challenge. Our forefathers endured so much pain and still strive in a society that treated Dogs and Cats better than Blacks. One of my experiences in dealing with racism was when I became a Commission Officer in the US Army as a 2nd lieutenant. I was tested daily by my peers and by my white soldiers whether I had the ability to supervise, manage or to lead them into battle. I was always questioned about my knowledge and my ability to plan a military operation. Senior non commission officers, i.e., sergeants didn't want a black officer in charge of them or telling them what to do. It was important that I stay abreast on all the military policies and procedures. I was always given mediocre task for my company. Although, I was very motivated to go above and beyond duty to get the job done.

However, I was graded less than my white counterparts. Therefore, I felt so isolated and all alone. So, I focused all my energy on taking care of my soldiers.

The Insurrection

The insurrection that occurred on January 6, 2021 was about the whites losing their power in America. Trump was the puppet for the uneducated rebels. These Caucasian people wanted people of color to continue to be in a servitude role in this society. Whites feared they would lose their white privilege. Blacks have always been a threat to them that is why they continue to keep us in a dark place in this world, uneducated, inequality, low wages, high interest rates, redlining and high tax rates. All this is done so blacks can keep on depending on them. It was Black African Americans that built this great Country. A place where our forefathers died fighting for freedom. Blacks have endured wars and escaped some of the harshest rule of law imposed on us by Caucasian people.

Slavery wasn't an accident; it was a form of control and power over the black race. In the military they took the black man's dignity; it is worse than you can ever imagine. They treated us less than a man. They feared us as leaders. All of this is a master plan to keep the black man in a dark place in society. Only a few people of color exceeded to the next level, most of them were light complexion, they used this to divide us. The whites used this division to pit us against one another and it worked. It is important that the younger people learn about their culture, so this tragedy will never happen again. This insurrection could have been prevented. The insurrection was a rebellion; the white people were willing to do anything to stay in power.

How do I feel being Black by Anjanette Phillips?

I have multiple feelings about being Black. I feel the divineness of my Black heritage within me, the creativeness, soulfulness, and Queen-like sense of my being. A black dress, car or jewelry is recognized as classic or elegant for a special occasion or event. Being a Black person, I feel the sting of hatred and prejudice because I am Black. A feeling of being devalued even by my own people. I feel like my strength is built from the brokenness of my foundation at birth, from the lack of opportunities to grow.

I feel Blessed being Black.

Thank GOD

On January 6, 2021, I can't remember what I was doing before I witnessed the insurrection. All I could do was stand still and watch. I felt unsafe and worried about my children. What could happen next? Did we have enough food and necessities in the house if we had to leave home unexpected? Who are these attackers and where did they come from? Are they, our neighbors?

Being Black Means… written from the heart of: Randi JaNay 7/1/2021

You asked me what it means to be black. Well, being black to me means, I am royalty descended from Kings and Queens not slaves. Being black to me means, my people gave birth to other nations. Being black to me means, I'm a trailblazer because my people created the blueprint of a rich and creative culture that is often imitated, but never duplicated. Being black to me means, God took his time to create something so divine. Being black to me means that I know knowledge gained becomes power obtained. Being black to me means, I should take pride that I come from people through history who have made waves, and moved mountains just to be seen, be heard, and be free. Being black to me means, I am part of an elite group. No matter how hard those who fear our strong presence try to intimidate us, we stand firm. We never break, because the only things we continue to break are barriers. Being black to me means, there's power within my heritage. What I inherited from my people besides my myelinated skin that can withstand the sun, hair that can defy gravity, and my defining features that set me apart from the rest is the strength and guidance of my ancestors that comes out when being put to the test. Being black to me means, that the suffering and pain those of my lineage endured in the past shall not be in vain. I will make it my responsibility that generations to come will know our roots were planted on a rocky foundation. But we are here to stay, and that **our people, black people**, overcame and shall sustain. I will instill in them pride for a brighter future. One day I will tell them what being black means to me and as they grow older, they'll think back on that day, and when the time comes that they are asked what being black means to them, I hope that in their own words, this is what they'll say.

How I feel being Black in America by Jake Pitchford

We don't value ourselves.

We do more to hurt our own race; this might be because we are underpaid. We don't show other folks we value each other. Whites don't recognize us as equal. We don't support each other like the other cultures.

All these black-on-black crimes, this shows a lack of respect for our own race.

The insurrection that occurred on January 6, 2021 was unpatriotic; these people did not love their country. It was just like the Civil War.

My thoughts about being Black in America by James Braswell

This younger generation seems to want to destroy what our forefather created. White people don't want to accept that we can reach the top and is good at what we do. Also, I remembered when I worked as a supervisor, the group leader used to harassment me every chance he got. It got so bad that the other employees started taking note. The other employees witnessed his abuse of power and they reported him. After that, he cooled down and was respectful. I was saddened when I witnessed the insurrection. Trump just would not accept the fact that he had lost. He wanted to be like the other dictators. It was a sad day for America.

Ada Harrison thoughts about being Black in America

Being Black is an advantage and disadvantage, we have to be double qualified compared to our white counterparts to get jobs.

Since George Floyd's death, some doors have been opened for discussion and things are getting better. Trump said what white people wouldn't say. That's what made him so popular.

White people want to continue to rule and stay in power at any cost. The massacres that occurred in history are examples of this.

Being Black in America by Mary Jo Darden

When I was young, I realized being black had it disadvantages. I struggled because I saw the disparities, the favoritism, and the way my brothers and sisters were treated all over the world. It hurt me deeply. When you are young, you don't understand why people are so unkind. I wanted the pain to stop, the idea of being white intrigued me. My father noticed I was struggling and one day, he sat me down and gave me the Talk. Not the Talk when you tell your children what to do when you are being stopped by the police, it was the regular talk between a father and daughter about casual things that was going on. He said, "Child be proud of your heritage, you came from beauty". Your mother is my queen. Stand and be proud! You are the essence of beauty. When I look at you, my child, I see love; I see all the beauty in the sky. That beauty shines with every smile. My father taught me to hold my head up high. He said "child never look away when you see someone white, look them straight in the eyes. 'This shows confidence and you fear them not. "My father was a great man! *He taught me to strive for the best and never accept anything less.* He told me, "Even if your job requires you to clean up feces, he said 'hold your head up high and pinch your nose and dish out 100% because God blessed you to have a job. "This resonated with me all my life. I was bigger than most of the kids my age, and shorter but

you would've thought I was ten feet tall because I strutted with my head high, I was a
queen in my father's eyes. My father said, "Child never look back." I was homecoming queen for two years at an integrated school. My parents taught me to put myself in front and center that meant not taking a back seat to anyone.

My mother told me, "Beauty comes only from the heart,' she said "being the prettiest is only a façade because beauty fades and the ugliness is exposed." Based on my parents' teachings, I was able to exhale. I took that advice to the heart because I never let my size and my fear hold me back from achieving my goal. I embraced my blackness and even though we still have hills to climb, I know, I come from the seed of love.

I know because why would they do everything in their power to stay in power and prevent us from exercising our right to vote.

It is hard being black; we are mistreated and hated only because we have black skin. But thank God for my parents, they taught me to value my self-worth. That's why I walk proud, I stand proud to be what I am, a black woman!

Also, when I saw the insurrection on TV, I thought to myself, those white folks done lost their minds. If that had been blacks acting in that manner, there would have been a mass shooting;

the blacks would never made it to **the finish line, the Capitol. That was disgusting.**

Being Black isn't easy by Dasia Moore

Has there ever been a time when being black was easy? Being black is hard, especially for black people. If you as a black person haven't experienced this, well you soon will. The Hardships of what "Our People" have been though aren't been discussed enough. From the harsh judgments we receive in the court system, with the scale tipped to favor the whites, it is all because of the color of our skin. Down to the negativity, we as blacks see this daily. It is that hate that is spewed from another human being, which is so mind boggling! This unkind world I live in today is biased; it is a place where whites think they are superior. Whites frown upon us, gossip, taunt us, and murder us for no apparent reason, other than false narratives. These baseless crimes have no merit, all this is based on the color of our skin. We are judged by the way we look, the way we dress and the way we present ourselves. And when blacks advance, the threat intensifies in their eyes. There has never been a consistent time in history where black people have had a peaceful gathering without police being called, soldiers and tanks being barricaded, but for what? Only for being Black. In discussion, on January 6, 2021, the attack on the Capitol will always be remembered in my mind as a day they wanted to steal democracy. It will not be remembered as anything positive. It won't be remembered for anything constructive, like much needed bills being signed into law to help protect black people. It will be remembered as a day that every single black person witnessing this knew exactly how it would go. We watched and we all knew that based on what we saw if that was a mass gathering of predominately black people, the outcome would have been different. Half the people would have gotten arrested, shot and most important of all, they wouldn't have made it to the Capitol steps. The jails would be filled with these undemocratic invaders.

We watched and saw a white mob destroy our government building and they celebrate the mayhem. The white mob didn't fear any repercussion and they were allowed to leave when it was over. Blacks would have been shot down like flies. I stated this to say, being black has never been easy from the slaves brought here against their wills and today, while the African Americans are supposedly living the American Dream, we continue to have to fight for any ounce of justice. We as blacks must continue to stand up, fight and believe in ourselves.

Because we know that whites will do whatever it takes to stay in power and revisit a time when blacks had no voice.

Now I ask you have there ever been a time when being black was easy?

My thoughts about being Black and what I experienced being a Black woman by Gloria Hill- Mckenny

I am a retired educator, I taught in Baltimore city public schools for 33 years. I grew up in a small town in Eastern North Carolina in the 50s and 60s.

I realized I was black at the tender age of about 8 or 9 years old. My mother took me to a restaurant to get a hot dog. We had to go to the back of the restaurant where there was a window to be served. We could not go inside.

I grew up down the street from white families. I could not play with them or go to school with them.

I quickly learned that people my skin color had to stay or mingle together and people with white skin mingled together. Therefore, learning my place in an institutional prejudiced racist, unfair society for black people. Some white people don't think there is racism because there is no racism FOR Them. They have not experienced racism like we have. **Some white people don't think racism exist because it doesn't exist FOR THEM. They are self-absorbed into their whiteness.**

As I grew up, and started to teach myself about African American History in the United States. I learned a lot of disturbing details that I was never taught in school. I learned that my ancestors endured slavery in the U.S. for 400 years. I learned that after the Emancipation was signed in 1863, Texas slaves were not freed until 1865. Thus, Juneteenth 2 years, later.

African American people still endured systematic residual left over oppression because of the effects of slavery:

Jim Crow Laws-Legalized segregation of public schools, public places, public transportation, restrooms, restaurants, drinking fountains, denial of equal opportunity to blacks

- **<u>Gentrification-</u> Buying up urban areas revitalizing them to sell to the rich and displacing poor people mostly African Americans**

- **<u>Massacres-</u>There are at least 33 other Massacres in the U.S that we don't know about other than the most well-known. (One** was, the Tulsa Oklahoma) This was to make sure that blacks did not gain generational wealth. The white mobs burned down

neighborhoods and communities for any reason, then enacted laws that were put in place to disadvantaged blacks.

- **<u>Red lining</u>- Denial of systematic services to certain minority neighborhoods and communities, and raising prices in those areas. Blacks could not get loans from banks to buy homes in 40s and 50s and part of the 60s. This law was enacted by Federal Housing Administration (FHA).**

- This created the wealth gap between blacks and whites. The way to build generational wealth is through equity in your home, good paying jobs and opportunities to businesses.

- Most blacks were locked out of these aspects of the American dream until 1968 (Fair Housing Act was passed.)

- **<u>War on Drugs</u>-Targeted black people (mostly black people) and put on track for the prison pipeline by the third grade**

- **Blacks are going to jail for petty crimes in record numbers**

<u>Gerrymandering</u>- changing the laws or changing boundaries to favor one party or class

of people. Packing black voters into a district (rezoning).

Ask yourself white people how are you helping to stop this devasting ball from rolling, so that racism and prejudice will not be passed down from generation to generation. This ball has been rolling for 400 years. Stop being self-absorbed in your whiteness and your white privilege!
Some white people might say I didn't do it, why should I have to pay reparations. I say to them, "your ancestors did it and you benefited from it and still to this day and time (from slavery and even today.)

Summary

I believe whiteness is routed in blindness and deafness to the struggles of black people because it is not real to them. They have not experienced it like we have. They experienced

1.   A bad day
2.   Bad luck
3.   Bad Boos

They don't understand our struggles. Black people experience all that and much more.

- Going to jail in large numbers for petty crimes

- Whites are not going to jail or getting harsh sentences for petty crimes

- Getting killed or shot down in record numbers by police I would like to thank Mrs.

Josephine Bridgers for asking me to write a passage to contribute to her book.

My feelings about being Black in America by Jevonte Williams

I feel that America is an unsafe place for us as blacks. Sometimes I feel like an orphan. America doesn't want me because I'm black and Africa isn't fond of me because I'm American. I feel like America is owned by the white man. Blacks have it hard trying to make it. They don't look at us as an average person; we either selling drugs or doing something illegal or trying to make our way to the top…

Being Black by Delicia R. Hilliard-Ross

My name is Delicia R. Hilliard-Ross, the niece of Josephine Hill Bridgers. My first realization of my skin color believe it or not was what one might not expect. I was born in the late 1960s; 1969 to be exact. When I started elementary school, it was 99% African American. My first experience of someone questioning or making a statement about my complexion, was my classmates wanting to know why I was so dark or black. I started cursing very early. It started to make me wonder was something wrong with me.

I'm glad I am a strong Black woman; a woman that has a strong personality and came from a strong background which gave me great confidence in myself. So, racism for some comes from all kinds of people and from all directions. It's hurtful enough coming from other races but when it comes from your own it takes on a whole different meaning. I have a cousin name, Larry Darnell Hill Jr. son of Aunt Josephine who once asked me, was everybody in our family dark? This led me to believe that he wasn't comfortable in his skin. When I realized that might have meant that our family wasn't rape by white men, they left us alone, it made me feel even more proud. Today, I am a very proud and prominent outstanding **DARK, BLACK AFRO AMERICAN Woman.** I don't have to worry about bruising easily, trying to tan or bleach. I know how to address and handle racism as it comes or happens to me from any directions or ethnic group.

The Set Up by Verner Avery

In 1972 my wife and I moved from Brooklyn NY in search for a better and less chaotic life style. So, we found this medium southern town

of about seventy-five thousand people. We did
not know anyone but that was ok, because we
liked the surroundings.

In Brooklyn we were designing and making
clothes part-time. So, we decided to open a small
boutique where we would be able to design
fashion for both men and women. The shop was
doing better than we expected. We were young
and worked 12 to 15 hours a day even on
weekends.

Now this was the first of 4 encounters with
the police but I am only mentioning two.

One day I started out to get a zipper and this
young black was coming so I came back into the
store. The young black man came in and looked
around for about ten minutes and didn't buy
anything. I stepped in the other room to tell my
wife I was leaving. When I opened the door I
saw this little yellow envelope directly in front of
the door, so I picked it up and opened it, wow, it
was marijuana, instantly, something told me to
hold it up in the air and walk it to this trash can
and drop it in.

I walked back to tell my wife what had
happened and the doorbell rang the person
walking in was a uniformed policeman. His
words to me were "I was just walking around to
see if everything was alright." In the previous
two and half years and the last forty-six years no
policeman has even made rounds.

On another occasion, a man walked in looking some-what homeless, he walked up where the ladies were sewing acting like he knew them and left, meanwhile, there were a detective already in the store, I thought to myself, that was strange.

Bettie Harrison being Black in America

I moved to New York in 1963 for better opportunities because there were little opportunities for Blacks in the south.

I went to New York and worked a sleep-in job; I stayed with my employer and was paid a salary to live in their home. I stayed a week and left early because the man of the house tried to seduce me; I declined his efforts and told his wife. After this encounter, the couple paid for my transportation to leave their home and I went to stay with my big sister. When I stayed in the south, I was ignorant to the fact that racism existed. Working the fields, I only saw black folks. When I went downtown, I only saw black folks. But, when I went up north, my eyes were enlightened, I saw racism for what it was, pure evil. I recalled when I worked as a cashier, I was afraid to charge the white folks the full price for items; the fear of white folks was so real to me that I under charged them and put my job at risk.

The manager had a talk with me about the money situation and I changed my thinking. I'll tell you another incident that occurred when I worked as a cashier in a super market, one day a white couple came in; they looked at me and then out of nowhere, they asked me this question. "If you had to sleep with any man in the world, who would you sleep with?" At first, I thought to myself, this was a crazy question. But the white couple waited for my answer, I opened my mouth and said, "Sidney Poitier." The couple looked bewildered; they probably thought I would pick a white actor. Why would anyone ask this question to a stranger? They didn't know that they were dealing with an unapologetic black woman who didn't mind speaking her mind after getting over my fear of white folks. Then I remembered going to my nephew's wedding, I was dressed in colorful attire; I had on a two-piece bell-bottom pant set, I was feeling very soulful, then a lady said, "you are bringing Africa here." I was bewildered. Some of us, not all, have regressed back into the Slave's Mentality. Pulling each other down, instead of lifting each other up.

I remembered thinking when I was taking a history class or just casual thinking, do black folks do anything besides play sports or be in the entertainment world? Then, I started reading, and there I found my passion, because I learned that not only did black folks invent things, they were much more than what the historians wrote about. Black folks were excluded in the history book, and most of the credit were given to whites.

After reading, I found out that we are inventors, scientists, doctors, lawyers, engineers and much more. I read everything that enlightened me, this thirst was all I needed to feel that we as black folks had some self-worth.

Today we still have to fight for any ounce of recognition. I have learned to embrace my black skin and be proud because not only have I lived my life; I believe our heritage is a vital part of our knowledge and I continue to keep that going being the president of my family reunion. Because that is what our forefathers were all about, uniting and staying together because at one point in time, we weren't valued as human beings. Some of our forefathers were auctioned off as someone's property and never got to see their family members again. I remembered what my parents taught me, that family was everything and keeping the communication going is a lifeline. That's why I worked hard for years as the President of the Harrison's Family Reunion. I revisited my thoughts about the slaves and how they fought to keep their family

together and I'll be damned their struggles will
not go in vain!

James B Parker and Lonnie B Parker

We grew up in loving families. Both of us
retired from education, but our thirst for helping
people did not retired. We decided to form our
individual businesses. My husband teaches
private lessons in music. Most of his students are
learning to play the instrument of their dream.
He is staying young and keeping his musical
skills sharp.
I started a Tutorial Clinic about fifteen years ago
for children who needed a little help in getting on
tract. We develop a bond that last until they
graduate from school. Some students start in the
elementary grades and come until they finish
school. The parents and I work together to keep
them motivated.
We love our business families

What I faced being Black in America, the author

About thirty years ago, I had applied and got accepted in the Nursing program. My kids were young. Back then, I lacked motivation so my studies failed tremendously, when I saw those huge books; I panicked. I couldn't focus. I didn't put in no work and my classes suffered to the point of me failing all my classes. I experienced racism from teachers; the white nursing students got away with things that black students would have been thrown out of the class. I heard it had gotten so bad that a couple of black students got together and reported some teachers for their racism and the teachers got in trouble but they didn't get fired. That is what I was told. I remembered when it was time for me to take a test, a test I never studied for, so again, I flunked.

In class, I remembered there were two sisters sitting beside each other; every test we had, they told each other the answers and the teacher saw them but did nothing. You guessed it; they were white. The two sisters would both study something different from what I was told and they would ace the test. I saw them also, but who you think the teacher would believe someone black that was flunking every test, or the two white students?

If I had only been motivated, but this luxury wasn't in my brain because I refused to study due to my preoccupation with the opposite sex.

But for some reason I could write, I've always been good about writing my thoughts on paper. One day, the teacher asked the students to write a paper, I didn't know what it was about, but when she read my paper, she looked bewildered. She pulled me aside and asked me point blank did I plagiarize my paper? I was hurt, because I always had the ability to construct a good paper. I told the teacher, no, and walked away offended!

Nevertheless, I flunked out of nursing school twice, because I refused to do my work and take my classes seriously. When you don't study what do you expect?

Years later when my children were grown, I focused on improving my quality of life by going back to school; it was hard, but my mindset did a huge turn around. This time, I studied. I put in work. Then I tried to get back in the nursing program since I was now focused, but ran into a road block, the Tease test. Now, the Nursing department required this to get in.

In all my classes, I was getting A's and B's. I was killing Biology with an A average. A lot of people was flunking out, white and black students, but this home girl was acing it. I was on fire with outstanding grades. But when I took the Tease test, it was odd, I got the same thing I got the last time I took it. This puzzled me. Finally, I asked the head of Nursing about the score, I said

"I can't understand why my score is the same as before." She just shrugged her shoulders. Then I said, why is a lot of white students getting into the program when I'm beating them in every class that I take with them, but yet, they can pass the Tease test and get accepted into the program? The head of Nursing looked like she wanted to crawl under the table. So, I decided to go another route, I majored in Medical Assisting. I did well until I took Math 140 and this single class tore my nerves to pieces but I got through it. I came out of that class with a D and I kissed the ground for that D because it allowed me to graduate. Nevertheless, it brought my grade point average down, but I graduated with an average of 89- or- 90.0 GPA, with an Associate Degree in Medical Assisting.

I ran into a problem my last year of college, due to the fact, I played around and flunked out of Nursing classes two times, this affected my grant, and I had no choice, but to stop going to college. I couldn't complete my Medical Assisting's classes, but an angel came through, named Mr. Wooten. A program he was involved with helped me continue my education, that's how I was able to get an Associate Degree in Medical Assisting. God truly opened that door.

When someone tells you can't get out there, prove to them you can! I did and so can you!

I remembered my last semester, I had to do my clinical and my back gave out. It was a disc in my lower back, it had flared up again. I had to do my clinical in the worse pain you could ever imagine, bending over because the pain was unbearable. But I continued to see the prize, I didn't let pain take away something I worked my brain to accomplish and neither should you.

We live in a world where interruptions can happen in an instant, so we should take the time to see through the eyes of others and supplement their failures by fueling the flames by inspiring others. I loved working as a CN1 but I saw too many things that troubled me, that's why I left a field that I liked to go into one that paid the bills. My main pet peeve was this: Lack of communication between the CNAs and the Nurses. What I mean by that is, some of the Nurses wouldn't answer the call bells unless the State was there. Some of the nurses would walk the halls looking for the CNAs neglecting to do what they were supposed to do, like answer the call bells. I told a nurse one night after she interrupted me while I was cleaning a patient, I said, "Can you please answer the call bell, just do it.!" I kid you not, I rolled my eyes because that made no sense at all to me!"

And to add insult to injury, when the patient's family members would come, they would tell on the CNAs but they didn't know, sometimes we had to tell the nurses that this patient need this and that because a lot of the nurses didn't do the basic in performing their job. That was frustrating.

One nurse told me point blank, "You are too smart to work as a CNA1." I looked at her and told her, "Someone has to take care of these people; and I just walked away.

I walked away from being a CNA because I witnessed an eye for an eye. I used this phrase a lot because, like I said before, we don't know when interruptions will occur and disturb our way of living. We take life for granted. A lot of rich women and men that had a life of luxury have succumbed to sicknesses and illnesses that landed them in nursing homes. One lady was so mean that the other white residents shunned her. They literally, shut their doors when she came on the hall. I remembered one time, a white resident asked me, "Why black people don't age like white folks." I didn't know the answer so I walked away shaking my head. There were times I just sat down and laughed; one time I was walking down a hall and a resident started chasing the staff with a deadly weapon, their wheelchair! We scattered to get out of his way ducking into rooms.

There was one resident in the nursing home who would get so hysterical when we told her it was time to take a bath. She acted like water was going to melt her body. She screamed and screamed; "I don't want to take a bath! "

I was underpaid for this demanding job; we were short staff a lot, with people having double clients that weren't allowed by the State. I had worked a lot of times being the only one on a hall of 32 patients. I got, zero help. I told the patients this so most of them helped me out by not ringing the bell and waited until I came in their room. I had to literally ask the nurses at the nurse's station to at least answer some of the bells. They looked at me like they were doing me a favor but it was a part of their job description as well.

Well, one day I had a meltdown, I wasn't going to work the halls with no help. There was a total of thirty-two or more patients that I was supposed to care for with no help. This time I refused because the same people kept on staying out, they were over was against the law to have that many patients to care for. I told the nurse this time, I just wasn't going to have it. I walked off the floor because they wouldn't provide me with any help. Nevertheless, I got fired for that rebellion act but I soon found a job at a neighboring nursing home. This nursing home was just as worse because people stayed out a lot there also. Good people got burned out fast leaving the no count workers pretending to care for the residents and providing them with poor care. That's the reason I left; I didn't like the way old people was treated. They were treated horrible.

One day in the evening, I witnessed a white CNA1 hiding in the closet of a resident because she refused to bathe the patient.

There were times when some of the people working that was supposed to feed the patients wouldn't give them their food. They would bring the tray back and say" the patient wasn't hungry". Sometimes I would take the tray and go and feed them and the patient ate all the food. Some jobs aren't for lazy people.

Some of the workers I worked with in the nursing homes weren't always kind to the residents, but my mother taught me to treat people like I want to be treated. One time I was working with another staff member and it came time to bathe a lady, for some reason she didn't want to bath this lady, I told her come on let's get started. She said, "why, she wouldn't even know if we gave her a bath or not." I said, "What!" Then I gathered my thoughts and told her. "She is a human being' and just because she is in a nursing facility that didn't mean she need to be disvalued as a human being. She worked with me that night because she knew I wasn't playing. I don't look at color because we all bleed red and have our own burdens whether you are white or black. There was one time I passed a resident's room and smelled an odor all too familiar, so I back tracked. I went in the room and a CNA1 was drinking a beer. I asked her, why she was drinking a beer in the patient's room. She said this, "look at her, she doesn't know if she is in this world or not? "I told her that it was all about respecting your job and the people you service". She got mad at me and told her friend. This caused a problem because working the halls you needed assistance getting the residents up and giving them a bath. When I asked her friend, she would disappear to the point I had to tell the Director of Nursing. She spoke to all parties and things seemed to get better.

This just happened recently, I was visiting my ex-father-law and a RN pulled up the same time I did, we went in to see my father-in-law. After a while we parted the same time, she begins talking to me about she had to go back to work sooner because she didn't have any money. She also said, her son stayed with her and had been in prison and he worked but didn't help her out. I told her, this is not good and she needed to become more firm or else when she died, he wouldn't know how to support himself. She seemed to be uplifted by what I told her. I also told her to pray because what we can't do, God can. I also mention to her that I had a daughter and two sons. A mother never stops worrying about their children. The nurse was white and I say this because, we faced the same things in life. But the bottom line is, we all want to live our life in peace. We hunger for enjoyment in a world that seemed to deny us the right to just grow old and swing our feet and thumbs. And sing old lullabies, this is what most people yearns for. I didn't look at this lady as a white lady, I looked at her as a human being that needed words of comfort because pain resonated in her eyes. I know because I have been there and done that. We have to empathize and realize we all have things that connect us than the things that divide us. Because at any given time interruptions could befall us: car accident, loss of income, become paralyzed, wind up in a facility

for the mentally insane or find yourself in a
nursing home, these are unforeseen incidents.
So, since we don't know what lies in the future,
treat people like
you want to be treated. That's a good motto to
stand by.

Other stories from the author

My oldest son had gotten into some legal
trouble with the law and was going before a
judge for sentencing. He was confident that the
judge would give him a light sentence until the
judge starting saying things like, "I heard you
have a Massarotti; I never seen but a couple in
my lifetime." The judge continued to list things
that my son had acquired through illegal gain.
My son said he started shaking because he knew
then and there that the judge was gonna throw
the book at him.

Then, after my son was sentenced, we
received another blow, a news reporter or anchor
reported on the news that my son was a snitch
and that's why his sentence was so light. This
could have been a death sentence for my son
going to prison. But because my son was black,
Mr. Cullen Browder thought it was his duty to
say that. The family was horrified. I didn't agree
with my son's actions, but I mourned for him

and worried about his safety. You never stop
been a mother; it's a 24/7 job. I emailed the news
reporter, Cullen Browder and he sent me a nasty
comment. I just wonder would he had done that
to a white person? This realization is real for
Blacks. Also, we as blacks gotta start supporting
each other; I remembered trying to get my talent
show together so I solicited a person that had
written a couple plays at her church. She had an
outstanding cast of people to choose from, so
one day, I asked her about using some of her
people in my talent show; she didn't say
anything. Later on, I bumped into her at a store
and I watched her as she avoided me when I was
about to walk up to her. This shocked me
because this person seemed so nice. I found out
later that she discouraged people who performed
in her shows not to participate in other people's
shows. Nevertheless, I was hurt. I walked away
with conflicting feelings. But to be fair, it isn't
my place to judge. This woman had worked with
my husband at school where he did janitorial
work. She had been very friendly before I talked
to her about using some of her people for my
event. This could've had a negative effect on me
but I was determined that I would pursue my
dream. I continued to chase after my dream of
having a talent show that consisted of raw talent:
a live band, ballet dancers, steppers, rappers,

skits, singers, soul food and etc. And to my surprise, I started getting people who supported me 100%. Now I am fortunate to have followers that come and support my shows.

The author recalled an incident that happened in the 1960ths, she was working on a tobacco harvester and someone asked for a drink of water, the boss lady who was white, gave the workers only one jar. Then someone else asked for water, that white lady was fuming mad now, she said "ya'll niggers have one jar to drink out of and that's it. We didn't like it but what could we do?

Also, on another occasion when the author was putting in tobacco, she and several others had to use the bathroom. She and the others got off the tobacco machine and walked down the path to the boss's house. They knocked on the door, the boss lady came looking like she had just gotten out of bed. When we asked her to use the bathroom, this lady acted like we had said we were gonna burn her house down; she made a face that scared the living mess out of us. Then she said with a harsh tone, "we don't allow niggas to use our bathroom. 'Go in the field where you belong." Even though, I had witnessed several occasions of racism, this one stung because I was young and I couldn't understand why they hated us

THE BRONZE PLANTATION AND MR. ED

On January 6, 2021 there was a violent attack on democracy, an Insurrection. The Insurrection was incited by Trump, number 45. Trump was defeated in his second bid for the White House. His mob attempted to demolish democracy because Trump couldn't accept the fact that he lost the election fair and square.

I watched CNN News, and saw the Insurrection happening before my eyes. This left me speechless. I watched on television and saw people forcing their way into the Capitol; they were destroying things, fighting the men in blue that they had previously claimed they supported. They chanted. They looted; this made me sick to my stomach. This act targeted Democracy at his core. And to let this madness continue for hours, this showed the level of what Trump's followers would go through to keep him in power.

And the fact that the people that were fighting to protect our elected officials, they were overwhelmed with a mob that couldn't be contained. This was another example of what racism looks like. The sad *thing about it, they actually thought a few people was going to overturn the election.*

We are the People!

THE BRONZE PLANTATION AND MR. ED

In my recollection in school, I can't remember any talks about blacks' and their contributions. That's why I didn't like my
history classes. History books mostly mentioned the contributions of whites leaving out major events in history that reflected our struggles, as well as our contributions. I just learned of the Tulsa Massacre in Oklahoma in the year of 2021. In all the years of my schooling, there was no mention of the Tulsa Race Massacre or it alternating name, known as the Black Wall Street Massacre. The massacre was started by a lie that caused an undisclosed number of blacks to die by hands of white mobs.

With The Civil War approaching, will there be *an eye for an eye and a tooth for a tooth?*

Preview of the author next book

Will it be the end of the Bronze Plantation with the Civil War approaching?
 Two Brothers, Massa Pee and Calvin, which side will they choose? Massa Pee and Calvin,

which son will the Grand Madame support? She was old as dirt but she wasn't about to give up her slaves without a fight.

Larry, William, Blue and Kelly which side will they choose? Massa Pee was mad, mad because people wanted to take what was his, his slaves. He was rich and he wanted to keep all that was his. He bought and paid fair price for them and now someone was trying to tell him what to do. He'd be damned, as long as he was white, he was going to fight for what was his. Sure, he had lots of money but, nothing was going to come out of his pocket to pay for property he owned. Hell no!

Well, Grand Lion, Massa Pee's wife, was smoking mad also because she had never washed her wrinkled butt in all her years of living and she wasn't going do it now. What the hell did she buy slaves for? It was their job to do the dirty work, wash her fragile butt. She wasn't about to lift her fingers to do their work, oh no! And what about the cooking and cleaning, she couldn't do that, she was a woman of privilege. She was super rich and her money dictated her worth, she owed it all to her momma. At an early age, her momma told her that she would never have to lift a hand to clean her butt as long as she had slaves. Why did they need rights? The slaves were fed well.

And then, there was Calvin, he loved his mother; he loved his brother, but this inhumane treatment had to stop; he had already chosen his side, the North. But he knew his brother, Massa Pee, would come at him with a passion, and sadly, his mother would be right beside him riding the white horse and scolding him while pretending to be a so-called Christian, but he knew better. With one hand she praised the Lord, and the other, she cursed and did foul things that was considered not fitting for a lady. But Calvin had awakened when he saw Kim being beaten, that's when he knew that slavery was dead wrong but he still ignored the signs until his heart melted and changed his whole thinking. Calvin now looked at slavery with a brand-new pair of eyes. He loved people for their own self-worth and not the color of their skin.

Calvin witnessed seeing the love the slaves displayed in their private hours; they loved like whites loved. They felt pain like he felt. He saw the love the slaves had for their children when they were sold and with every lynching, he heard their screams. Calvin, son of a renowned slavery owner now was liberated; he fathered four children by his white wife, he had two boys and two girls.

Calvin also had a son by a slave; his son's name was William. Calvin's wife was from England and her parents taught her that slavery was pure tee evil but she didn't say anything. Especially, since her family was part of the Underground Railroad and had housed many runaway slaves. She couldn't understand why slavery was even permitted. What type of people would do this to human beings anyway? She didn't understand! But she was behind, Calvin and she had accepted his son, Blue. Now, the Civil War was approaching, would it be a*n eye for an* eye, a tooth for a tooth? William, Kelly, and Blue, you know what side they were on. A reckoning was about to happen now that the Civil War was approaching. Larry was ready to put a knife in his own brother's back, but will Blue just stand by? Oh no! Brother against brother, father against son, and mother against her own child, who would be victorious? And the Grand Madame, she couldn't wait, the anticipation was exciting to her. She was ready to ride her favorite horse, the horse of doom that she rode when she wanted to silence her opponents. She taught the Grand Lion everything she knew about what to do when a rebellion rose up against her. Blue, was a mix breed, he was willing to return to fight for all the slaves whose voices had been silenced? Hell yeah! What about

William? Yes, he was ready; this was something that was worth fighting for. Glory was within his reach; it didn't matter whether he returned or not. It was his duty, because his mind reflected back to the time when they berated beautiful young black Quinita and took her innocence while laughing about it. After shaming her, it was his mission to right the wrong. It meant, an eye for an eye.

"Yes, I will fight, William said. 'I will fight for the rights of my fellow slaves. Fight for the Nation in which we were bought and sold." He recognized that this burning spirit compelled him to do right by his fellow slaves which were still considered commodities and still whipped and chained! What about Tom? The white laborer who raped poor Quinita. Well, he was ready to destroy William, after all, William cut his little itty-bitty manhood off that was used to rape young slaves of their virginity.

Tom was ready, he wanted retribution. But was he ever gonna face William? Time would tell. Secretly, Tom feared William but Tom had the South behind him, so he strutted proudly, "I am gonna get that black bastard!

Ha, Ha!

William, on the other hand, dreamt of a day when he would come face to face with Tom. Before he left, he didn't have much time to give

Tom the full extent of his rage. This time he would make sure that Tom felt the fire and the fury of what he had done. Tom would never forget that a black man destroyed him and paid him back for all the young slaves he had violated to suit his ego. Oh, yes, he was gonna give him a good old fashion beating that he'd never had before. Tom's wife had left him; she ran off with a young overseer half her age, after all, Tom couldn't do anything anyway, long before his little itty-bitty pee wee was cut off.

But what about Kim, will she ever see her children she had by Grand Madame's husband, and the one she had by a slave? She wept every night for this opportunity.

But before the Civil War sides had been drawn. Calvin was leaving his haven in England and returning home and he had forces behind him. Massa Pee had gathered all the top guns, all these men had so much money and they were willing to pay whatever price to protect what was theirs, the slave trade. Blue, on his journey to freedom ran into a major problem, he almost got himself lynched. I will wet the reader's appetite. I left out critical points about Blue's quest for freedom. Well, Blue was almost there but before he could board the train, a plantation owner spotted him. Blue, however, was able to give his son to a conductor and the lady was able to hide the boy under her huge garment. Blue started fighting like hell because he knew it meant his survival. He cornered one of the fanciest looking white men and gave him a beat down; he had the strength of ten men the way he was throwing them around like hay. He was about to grab another man when he saw several weapons pointing directly at his head. The men gave him a good old fashion beat down. But Blue endured the pain, one was about to shoot him but the other fancy dressed man pulled him back, saying, "he belongs to Massa Pee." We gotta do it the proper way. When the morning set, ya'll can lynch this no count bastard. There, unbeknownst to Blue, he had someone in his corner, the local sheriff. He was Maylene's first-born by Blue's father, Massa Pee. The sheriff recognized Blue right away but, pretended he didn't know him. "Come here bastard!" The sheriff ordered. He grabbed Blue and hit him with his gun. Oh boy, there's gonna be a lynching when day sets in. Blue didn't know anything about Maylene or her son. But the sheriff had sent word to his mother that they had found Blue, that same night, Maylene contacted Massa Pee. The next day a lynching was scheduled, but somehow, Blue had been shot in the middle of the night by guess who, Maylene's son and a body was dangling on a rope hanging from a tree near the local saloon. The slave's face was unrecognizable but his hair and skin coloring were the same as Blue's. The sheriff sent word for Massa Pee to come and claim his slave, after all, he was from the Bronze Plantation. Massa Pee came, and when he saw the body, he cut it down. He inspected the corpse and turned and spit on it. Yes, it's that no count slave that ran away; he strutted off and left Blue's body in the street. All the town went wild, they had finally caught the slave that had alluded them for months. Maylene had come to town, she and her son walked away hand and hand, she patted her son's head. But was Blue dead, no, his father, Massa Pee had come and saved his son; he didn't have the heart to see his son get killed. He was coldblooded, but there was something about this boy that he couldn't shake loose. Massa Pee believed in an eye for an eye, but today, Blue was on his way to a safe haven and Kelly had been enlisted to help Blue escape again.

{Mr. Ed}

Mr. Ed's story mirrors so many stories; I watched him humble himself when he was called a boy when he was a grown man with young children. Mr. Ed knew it was the white man's insecurities that targeted African Americans, but nevertheless, it was hurtful. Yes, he was broken because of his addiction to alcohol, but he came from a long line of strong men. Mr. Ed's strength came from his wisdom. He passed down his wisdom to me, Josie. He fought to protect his wife and children, and for that, I loved him dearly. He was a descendent of one of the most heroic slaves of all, William. Born into slavery, William fought to reclaim his name, letting freedom ring and ring, after all, he was a Man not a Boy!

Being Black by Calvin Bridgers

My parents died at a young age. Being black in the 70s was very hard but before my parents died, they taught me to be responsible. I was around twenty-four when my mom died, and this was a devastating lost to me.

I learned at an early age that my skin color dictated the trials I would have to face and the fight I would have to conquer in order to establish my place in society. I realized that I would have to fight for every penny to secure what I needed to survive in this prejudice world that I live in.

I started working with my dad, and at first, we started off doing a lot of yard work. Later, I worked in a factory for a while.

Later on, I started working in the school system. I worked my job diligently without any problems for years. Then I encountered a racist principal, she taunted me until the point I had to quit my job. A job I had worked for almost twenty-five years. Every time I finished one job; she was on me to do something else. I knew my job well and was a good worker because I received awards for having one of the cleanest schools in the county. But this wasn't enough for this racist principal. My nerves were shot, so before I said something that I would've regretted

I quit and walked off. After I quit, the school had a meeting and the parents demanded accountability for the principal's action towards me and the parents demanded that I be hired back because the school wasn't the same and the school looked a wreck. Nevertheless, the principal was reassigned instead of getting fired. The school was composed of 99% of Blacks; they weren't having this blatant disrespect from a principal that caused a loyal employee to quit. The parents protested and action was taken. I took back my power, I refused to be disrespected by a racist; my parents' voices rang in my head, child never hang your head in shame. STAND UP!

Also, I remember when I decided to buy a house and when I applied, my application was accepted. This is from working a janitorial job for years and establishing good credit. The house I acquired, one of the teachers that worked at the school I worked had applied for it but she was denied because of her credit score. I said this because it doesn't matter the job title you have, it's all about managing your money.

Rosa Parks by Josephine Bridgers

Ole grave I fear you not.
I come to you flesh and bones with only the
armor of God's words.
The rotten stench of fear consumes me but I
refuse to let it consume or stain my thoughts.
Misguided and abused, for what? This law of
the land rains down favoritism; who gave them
the right to ask me to give up my seat?
I'm a grown woman not a child.
Is segregation the right course for men and
women to be divided and shepherded before they
are slaughtered?
This is a form of captivity every time I see a
sign, blacks not allowed.
For hatred to spew from their lips, these
pretentious fools have no integrity.
Segregation only kindles more hate.
Hatred has no power over me, go away I say!
Go hide in the threads of clothing meant for
cowards! I will not be pampered nor will I
entertain my silence any longer
No longer a beaten down participant, I, Rosa
will become the heir of my own fate. A fate
bought with Blood, Sweat and Tears!
I hunger for justice. If segregation separates us,
then I must demand change!

Recognizing, this honor is not for me to claim, this Glory remains and shall remain with the highest, God!

I come to you, my friend; just a meager woman with my Bible

Serenity empowers me, it revives my soul

Standing on the grace of hope for all men and women that have been silenced

I say no more! I will no longer be disenfranchised by a corrupt system. I refuse to continue to give up my seat for another human being to ride while I stand up and bite my tongue.

I lift my eyes up and said a silent prayer.

Oh no, I have no desire to be a saint. Only to be treated with respect!

This is another observation by the author

The author was dropping off one of her client's daughters to school when she observed this: the little girl in the back seat noticed her two classmates, she yelled out the window. I looked back and noticed the two white girls were waiting for her. When she got out, she greeted the two little white girls with a hug and they walked hand and hand to their classes. Awe, I thought, why can't the world be like that, looking through life through the lens of children?

It is my dream one day to help create a safe haven for abused and neglected children.

After seeing so many cases, it is my long-life desire to help children who have been abused and neglected by creating a safe haven. This will help them build their self-esteem and help them heal their wounds.

Also, another one of my life dreams, is to help push legislation for grandparents' rights in North Carolina. In North Carolina, grandparents don't have any rights.

I personally know the pain of going through challenging things when literally my hands were tied behind my back. If the grandparents didn't step up in most cases, there would be more causalities...

The talk by JJB

Boy: Momma I was stopped by the police
Momma: lord no, no
Boy; MOMMA they called me out of my name; they hand-cupped me while they laughed in the street
Momma: No, my child, No!
Boy: momma after they disregarded my rights, they told me to take my ragged tail home!
Momma:
NOOOOOOOOOOOOOOOOOOOOOOOOOOOOO
OOOOO
Boy: momma, why didn't you sat me down and give me that special talk?
Momma: child do ya remember when I came in your room late one night and told ya the hours had come
Boy: yes, momma
Momma: I knew that the fall had arrived
Boy: what ya mean momma
Momma: son you are a black man in a white man's world
It's time for you to watch every step you take and humble yourself if you are stopped by the police
Boy: but momma I thought you were half-sleep to say the fall was about to come, it made no sense

Momma: I said that to prepare you my child for this

Boy: but momma what is the fall?

Momma: all your life my child you will be measured by a stick

Boy: a stick

Momma: You were stopped my son for no probable cause, this my son is the beginning of the fall

Boy: what

Momma: son, da, da days have come, roll your sleeves up higher and release your pride in the sky! This my child will determine whether you live or die.

Boy: oh, I think I understand momma. It takes a man to be humble because when they were calling me out of my name, I smiled and said in my mind, God is with me, then the fear regressed in the sky. I remembered what you taught me, saying, "son, you don't need a weapon to show your hand, with the reigning prince of peace because God's words will always stand"

Momma: that's right, my child

Boy: I was polite momma, and I kept my cool

I had my phone in my hand really to film in case of the fall

Then I remember what you told me, it came to me clearly, it was like a song singing in my ears, if we walk without God, we don't stand a chance

Momma: that right my child because, if you are black or brown, you need to hear the talk to survive!

Boy: Momma, muddy waters drenched my eyes, sweet defeat enticed my cheeks but momma, I didn't bow my head in shame, I smiled and said, my momma taught me my name at a tender age. She taught me pride every day before I stepped out the front door. "She said, "child never bow your head in shame, you my beautiful child that happen to be brown and you are special child because of God.

Boy: Momma, these people are cowards hiding behind a badge of shame; their badges are supposed to protect the public but they kill as if they are playing a war game. But with that said, I raise my chest with pride, it was that pride that allowed me to be alive. The love you instilled in me, momma, I could feel it thumping in my chest. It was that love that kept me going amidst the unrest. But amidst the chaos, I here to say, there wouldn't be another black fallen by a coward's hands today. It is my hope that all parents, look and listen, and take the time to talk to their children on how to act when they have an encounter with law officers, sometimes your actions will dictate whether you live or die.

Sadly, we still have to face the white man rage because he can't contain us and put us back into a box

I Harriet Tubman by Josephine J. Bridgers

I rather had died in my mother' s womb with a belly filled of dreams than to be powerless to fight a cause that would've made my forefathers scream out, how long, how long, my Lord? The stench of slavery pollutes my thoughts drenching my heart with disgrace.
Caging men and women like dogs while professing to love God is an insult to God's integrity and a disgrace to his name.
If we allow this crooked cycle to go on, then we to add more notches to the chain!
Where is the victory, my Lord?
Is it tucked away in the Massa's hut?
Innocence people beaten, shamed and killed; this heavy price tag for freedom isn't theirs to own or claim! But whether I succeed or not, it is my fate to prepare the way for the next
Warrior waiting to be born. I'm anxious.
I scratched my body until it bleeds trying to remove the saliva from the Massa's spit
Silence calls my name from the grave

Only cowards, not men enslave and promote this type of ignorance. My soul cries out Freedom! Freedom! Why do they want to take what is not owed to them? They can bruise my flesh. But this burning desire for freedom echoes deep inside my brain saying it's time, "Harriet, raise your voice and make your stand!" Even if they dehumanized me and treat me less than a dog, to satisfy their depraved appetites, it is their shame to bear on their grave not mines.

Because what's born from the fruits of Love can't be contained in a cage. Remember this, I'm just a messenger tilling my way in the rain!

Slavery written by Jamey L. Wilkins

A slave is a slave is a slave. No matter how fancy you dress him up, no matter how articulate or educated he may be; a slave is still a slave. It's a bit deeper than just the "slave mentality" rhetoric that some feel by acknowledging its existence means they are not a victim of it. The word slave brings to mind uneducated men transformed into beasts of burden. It brings to mind lynching, torture, rape, racism at its pinnacle. Slavery brings to mind whips and chains, plantations, cotton and of course "Massa." Just the word slave itself makes you think of a torn clothed, dirty barefoot black-man; it makes you think of Kunta… Kunta Kinte. It makes you think of everything you could not possibly be; it also makes you feel as though it could never happen to you. Like if you were alive back then you would've fought tooth and nail for your God-given right. Well, the reality is you would not have, you would've woken yo' black ass up, picked cotton, shined Massa's boot with your spit and then danced a jig if he told you to. You would've broken a sweat hoping you'd find favor enough in his eyes to the scraps that they discarded as unworthy of being eaten. You know how I know, because you do it now. You are not built from the same fabric as Nat Turner, hell you aren't even on the same wavelength as Harriet Tubman. She had more nuts than you'll ever have. Black Man. You sit back and watch as police officers come to your city, your hood, your home and beat your brothers, cousins, son and fathers senseless. Why? Because you are a slave. You get locked due to a direct correlation to environment and its lack of necessities but abundance of drugs and weaponry and then even though in the streets you couldn't get a job worth working, you are forced to work for 40 cent a day in order to get gain time or just because they want you to work per the 13th amendment for it, if you do not you will spend your time in solitary confinement. Why! Because you are a slave. You work on an average job twice as hard in the lowest departments for not even half as much then are the first to call your supervisor (Massa) when a fellow worker or customer takes some of the product he helped make, produce, grow or package for himself hoping he'll promote you to a higher position (or the house) or give you something extra. Why? Because you are a slave. "Oh no, not me, you say, "I have graduated college. I'm an entrepreneur; I own my own business. I definitely am not a slave!" Okay smarty-pants, who gave you your education and taught you what they wanted you to know? Who allowed you to get your college grant/loan? Who allowed you to incorporate your business? Who do you pay rent to? To set up shop on their land? Think about it. Think about all the people who did/do the exact same things you have an did not reach the same results. You're a minority; the majority does not succeed. Now ask yourself what it is about you that made you succeed. Now ask yourself what it is about you that made you successful. What did they see in you that made them decide to allow you to advance? Please don't fool yourself by thing you are smarter, worked harder or are special. Nah, I'll tell you what they saw in you, they saw a special kind of slave. You see you are just a developed slave, what back in the days would've called an overseer. You are the slave that does not need physical chains because they taught you to be so smart that you are too stupid to run. They know you'll prevent another brother from escaping even put your own life at risk to keep them straight. All while Massa sits back and gets fat from the sweat of your brows. It is exactly this system that makes you a slave. The trick is simple but effective. One man with one gun with one bullet can lay down fifty people. All he has to do is pull it and shoot one person to emphasize who has the power. The rest will not move out of fear of being the next person shot. Now turn that negative scenario inside out to its positive counterpart (knows and understand that Massa knows they both can have the same results) one group of people can have the same results) one group of people can keep a larger group of people in check or let me stay docile by allowing one to succeed. They only have one opening to fill but just the sight of that one person making it will give hope to the Massa making them feel that if they try hard enough or if they just do the right thing then they can also make it when in all actuality as in the first scenario, they were only one. To keep everyone filled with hope, every blue-moon they'll search for another potential developed slave who they already know will be so happy to have been chosen he'll only be an extension of them because this Sambo will bojangle, snitch or whatever it takes to stay in their good graces. Then in time he will forget that he was one of subdued crowds, he will look down on them, criticize, berate and hate them for not achieving what he achieved. He will take on the traits of the Massa and hold them all at gunpoint for him. The crowd will then look at him as an Uncle Tom, as house nigger, when ninety-nine percent of them would be him if given the chance. They'd love to be the unshackled slave not realizing in both cases they are still a slave a slave is a slave is a slave. I know some of you reading this may think I'm talking about you, well I will save you the time, I am! I want you to know I am talking about you, you ignorant, brown nosing…. Coward. You are not wiser nor did you make better decisions. The lesser of two evils is not a decision. To choose to

not commit a crime but starve is not upstanding,
righteous. Nor good. It's being stupid. To accept
less than what you are supposed to have been not
a wise move it's capitulation. Look at the maze
surround you; it seems like each turn is a dead
end and if not, it's filled with trials and
tribulations but one of them allows you to live.
Nah, there are more than one that offer survival
but what kind of survival? If you have to give up
one freedom to get another, that's not life, that's
slavery! How about you stop going through the
maze and go through the maze. Just bust this
whole system to pieces and stake your claim.
That's freedom. Anything less is slavery. It irks
me when someone has the tenacity to come out
of their mouth and say" Well you shouldn't have
got locked up. What is that supposed to mean?
They don't see that I am…their cousin, brother,
nephew, uncle, father. Husband, or son. They
don't commend me for having the heart to fight
back. They don't see that I am what they
celebrate now but called stupid in the past. All of
their civil rights leaders that they venerated today
because they gave them the modicum of air that
they call freedom were criminals, lawbreakers.
But when I do it, when I resist, when I stand
firm, I am a fool. Well, I'd rather be a fool than a
wise slave any day. Maybe one day they will
understand. Maybe one day they will venerate

me but I doubt you will. YOU know why? Cause
you're a slave

This piece is solely the opinion of the
writer; however, it has some elements
that screams out, yes, Speak on Brother!
The author disagrees with some of the
writer's analogies, but on a whole, this
piece is brilliant.

Glory, Glory by **Josephine Bridgers/ Zakiy Ahmad McLain**

It's about the people unable to tell their story. So, I speak what I speak not taking away from God's Glory. I had a dream just like Martin Luther King. But my dreams flourish in my head. Saying, "stop all the killing!" Families are losing their loved ones every day, that's why we must humble ourselves and pray. If freedom rang, let all men and women gain. Let's stop the wage gap because it is a sham. This method is used to disenfranchise blacks from pursuing the American Dream. Freedom is an energy that invigorates our spirit; it empowers us to rise up and outwit our enemies. Think about all the trailblazers that fought and died. Fear stared them in the face yet they continued to strive. They had the rhythm of hope dancing in their bones. That what the white man couldn't take away because it was inborn. The spirit of God kept them warm. Let his victory spew down from the mountaintop where liberty is a delicacy, a prize afforded to everyone. We've come too far to revisit the words of Malcolm X, "by any means necessary." This to me, means you throw me a blow, I will come back with a blade. In his time, Malcolm practiced this saying faithfully. In the spirit in believing, let us not forget another trailblazer, Rosa Parks. In the midst of hate, she rose tall outshining her enemies; she witnessed the Glory of God because she could've been another casualty. Her Faith in God kept her alive despite all her adversaries. She visualized the lamb playing with the lion; this luxury is for all God's children seeking the pride. This is a question I pose to you. Why when black people walk, they must keep their hands up? Is it because any signs of defiance they would be laying in the dust? Martin represented peace, but never got none. He passed his vision to Stacey Abrams and she ran and never looked back, but guess what, they tried to assassinate her character but she did not budge. We were once slaves and never got paid; now they're afraid that one day we will reach the mountaintop. That's why they solicit crabs in the barrel to pull us back in the soil. These thoughtless people don't realize they are being used; they are just another Uncle Tom, grinning and shining shoes. And we must not forget, Michelle Obama, her speech at the Convention was brilliant. "I wake up every morning in a house that was built by slaves and I watch my daughters, two beautiful, intelligent, black young women Playing with their dogs on the White House lawn. "She refused to let her legacy be perceived as an angry Black Woman. Now, our first President, Obama, they fought him tool and nail and when they came low, he whipped out his executive privilege, saying I aint playing with you. And if that wasn't enough, he had an ace in the hole, his beautiful Black wife, Michelle Obama. He was the only President in history that was asked to show his birth certificate. But to show his great character, he passed the baton to his adversary with dignity and pride to number 45. Number 45 did everything in his power to criticize and divide. He rode his white privilege throughout the White House causing people to scramble for some sanity but there was none.

Ultimately, he left a disgraced leader due to his lies. Jealously, jealousy, this plagues us. Retribution will never be enough. They burned down our cities and wiped it from our history books. But there were survivors and they recounted the events that led to the massacres. Now they using the Critical Race Theory to wipe out their wrongs. But, they can't. A true leopard shows who they are. Now you have people taking medication to numb the pain. No fame no name but is it good enough? But one day, surely, *Glory will come. One day we will see the coming of the Lord*

Faith keeps us strong; we will continue to fight for equality until the work is done!

She led the way, so that they can continue to lead...